My Brother the Enemy

R.P.G. Colley

ISBN-13: 978-1499573848
ISBN-10: 1499573847

R.P.G. Colley

Rupert Colley was born one Christmas Day and grew up in Devon. A history graduate, he worked as a librarian in London before starting 'History In An Hour' – a series of non-fiction history ebooks that can be read in just sixty minutes, acquired by Harper Collins in 2011. Now a full time writer, speaker and the author of historical novels, he lives in Waltham Forest, London with his wife, two children and dog.

Fiction:
My Brother the Enemy
The Black Maria
Anastasia
The Woman on the Train
This Time Tomorrow
The Unforgiving Sea
The White Venus
The Red Oak

History In An Hour series:
1914: History In An Hour
Black History: History In An Hour
D-Day: History In An Hour
Hitler: History In An Hour
Mussolini: History In An Hour
Nazi Germany: History In An Hour
Stalin: History In An Hour
The Afghan Wars: History In An Hour
The Cold War: History In An Hour
The Russian Revolution: History In An Hour
The Siege of Leningrad: History In An Hour
World War One: History In An Hour
World War Two: History In An Hour

Other non-fiction:
The Savage Years: Tales From the 20th Century
A History of the World Cup: An Introduction

"A superbly written and acutely observed book, with well-rounded characters and convincing dialogue, while the tension and pace are perfectly judged."

"This book not only grabs your mind, but grips your heart and won't let go! Grab the tissue box and hold on."

"A tale with a sense of epic grandeur despite its brevity."

"Heart wrenching."

"Well-drawn characters and the ending is especially clever."

"Packs a considerable punch."

"It all adds up: turbulent historical setting, vivid descriptions, realistic and likeable central character, page-turning excitement, heart-stopping denouement, passion, heroism and betrayal."

My Brother the Enemy

Rupertcolley.com

PART ONE:

**A village near Berlin,
June 1936**

Chapter 1: The Forest

Stumbling into the forest was like entering a cool room. With their hair damp with sweat and their shirts sticking to their backs, the thirteen-year-old twins blinked as their eyes adjusted to the relative darkness. What a relief to be out of the sun and the suffocating heat of the heavy morning.

The boys sat down on their familiar resting place, a weathered tree stump, and shared a bottle of water, their chests heaving, having walked two kilometres in the heat across the exposed expanses of the wheat fields.

'She might not be there,' said Peter, his words coming between short breaths.

Martin gave him one of his withering looks that always caused Peter to regret speaking his mind. 'Course she will,' he said, taking another swig of water.

'If you say so.'

'Of course. She was there yesterday, wasn't she? So the chances are she'll be back today. Especially on a day like this. You don't have to come. Go home now; I don't care.'

'No, I want to.' Having come this far, Peter wasn't going back and Martin, of course, knew that. Pushing the cork back into place, Martin put the bottle into the sack and, handing the sack to Peter, rose to his feet. Peter would have preferred a couple of minutes more but knew there was little point in protesting.

Martin led the way purposefully along the dry muddied path, zigzagging past the oaks and maples, his head bowed in concentration. He was eager to get there, Peter knew, eager to relive the excitement of the previous day. White rocks broke through the earth; the sun poured through the leaves making mottled patterns on the ground. Even the forest seemed quiet, too exhausted by the heat to come to life, but somewhere a magpie squawked. Peter followed, relieved to be out of the sun, focussing on the boots in front of him and the small clouds of dust billowing up in the wake of his brother's feet.

Martin was the eldest of the two, as his brother frequently reminded him – born a whole thirty minutes earlier. And for the sake of that half hour, Martin had claimed the role as the older brother. Forever domineering, forever scornful, Martin was the leader. Where Peter hesitated, Martin jumped. This morning's expedition was typical – Peter didn't want to go; either it'd be a waste of time because she wouldn't be there, or somehow their father would find out, and then there'd be hell to pay. But Martin, always believing lightning could strike twice, was determined. And Peter, more worried about what he *might* miss than the possible consequences, followed suit. As always.

4

They started on the gentle incline down towards the lake where the forest thinned out and the mud-impacted ground was potholed with small stones. Solitary bushes of thistles sprung from the ground. 'God sake, hurry up,' said Martin without turning. 'She could be there by now.'

Somehow, Peter doubted it but kept his reservations to himself. The slope became steeper as they approached the clearing. As the path evened out, Martin began running, heading for the fallen tree, just yards away.

The twins lay on their stomachs, their heads against the crumbling wood of the hefty trunk, catching their breaths, relieved to have reached their destination. They peered over and scanned their eyes across the silvery lake shimmering in front of them, its waters reflecting the sky. A kingfisher swooped down and skirted across, disturbing the glass-like surface. Whether it caught anything, the boys didn't notice. They were too busy looking for her.

'She's not here,' said Peter, not sure whether to be disappointed by her non-appearance or pleased that he'd been right after all.

'She'll come. We'll just have to wait.'

They'd been waiting for almost an hour in silence, lying on their backs. Peter would have dozed off after the exertion of having got there, but thoughts of his father kept troubling him. If their father knew what they were up to, he'd go mad. Not that he needed much of an excuse. Ever since the Nazis had exiled the family to this far-flung village, Father had been angry. Their father's sense of humiliation, combined with his new-found love for alcohol, had changed him. If the twins weren't the cause of this perpetual anger, then it was their mother. For Peter, he liked it out here, away from the city, having his brother all to himself, but given a choice, he'd go back to the old life where his father had self-respect and love for his children. The Nazis had achieved what even the Depression had failed to do – they'd broken him.

*

'She's here!' Martin's excited whisper brought Peter back to the present.

He twisted onto his belly, his heart beating, and looked over the trunk. Yes, there she was, laying out her blanket on the sandy ground at the edge of the lake. She was dressed the same as yesterday – a sky-blue skirt that fell to her knees and a lemon-yellow blouse; the light colours contrasting with the darkness of her hair.

'She's beautiful,' said Martin, perhaps a little too loudly, for she turned round and the twins ducked down beneath the trunk as if being fired upon.

'She's seen us,' whispered Peter.

'I don't know.'

A minute or two passed and nothing happened. With his hands resting against the trunk, Martin slowly lifted his head above the wooden parapet. 'Oh my God.'

'What?' said Peter, fully knowing by the tremor in his brother's voice that, at last, their efforts were being rewarded.

She'd already slipped out of her skirt and was removing her blouse, the yellow fabric peeling away to reveal the whiteness of her skin. And so there she was, wearing nothing but her brassiere and large off-white knickers. Again, she looked round, making sure she was alone, and quickly removed her underwear. Peter's breath quickened as he absorbed the sight of the naked woman, trying to commit the image to memory – the marble paleness of her skin, the forbidden triangle of black hair, the small, pointed breasts. She strolled to the lake's edge, paused a moment, and then stepped into the water, which Peter knew, even on such a hot day as this, would be icy cold. With a sense of disappointment, he watched as the water took away her nakedness until finally, she dived gently in.

'She can't half swim,' he said.

'It's not her swimming we've come to see,' said his brother, turning away and lying against the trunk. 'Keep watch and tell me when she comes out again.'

The sun had moved and the boys found themselves under its direct glare. Peter kept watch, as ordered, but in no time she'd swum so far out, she'd disappeared from view. He rested his chin against the trunk and, like his brother, looked forward to her coming out again. Occasionally, he'd see a distant splash of water, each time further away. After a few minutes, he felt drowsy, the heat sapping his concentration and, eventually, his enthusiasm.

*

He'd no idea for how long he'd been asleep when he was woken up with a start by a familiar voice. 'Hello boys, what are you doing here?' Martin jumped too, both of them blinking against the sun.

'Monika!' squeaked Peter.

'What are you up to?' she asked, her eyes narrowing.

'Nothing,' said Martin, recovering his composure.

'So why do you both look so guilty?'

'We were asleep, that's all,' said Martin. 'Now go away.'

'Shan't. Why should I?'

'Sod off or I'll hit you.'

'Try it.'

Peter knew his brother was only making matters worse. He glanced back over the tree and could see the movement of water coming back towards them. They didn't have much time. 'We have to go now,' he said, rising quickly to his feet.

Fortunately, Martin took his cue. 'Yeah, we were off anyway.'

'You're a long way from home,' said Monika.

'So are you,' retorted Martin.

'I've come to find my sister.'

'You have a sister?'

'Yes. Is that someone in the lake?'

'No,' said Peter, perhaps too quickly.

'Yes it is.'

'We're going. You coming?' said Martin.

Peter looked back – the woman was emerging from the water, her wet skin glistening in the sun.

Monika eyes widened. 'It's my sister. She's not got any… You, you two were–'

'No we weren't.'

'You were, too.' Her voice rose with excitement. 'Quickly, she'll see us.' She ran round the side of the slope towards the trees, the twins following. Once inside the density of shade, the three of them stopped. Monika began laughing. 'I can't wait to tell her.'

'Shut up,' said Martin.

'You peeping-toms,' she screeched, pointing, her arm shaking as she laughed. 'Just wait…'

Martin's face reddened. 'Just wait till what?'

'Your father—'

Martin suddenly leapt towards her, an expression of ugly intent on his face, and slammed Monika against a tree. She squealed as her back scrapped against the jagged bark. Thrusting his face close to hers, their noses almost touching, he said, 'Listen, you stupid little cow, one word, just one word—'

'Martin, stop it, you're hurting me.'

'And I'll hurt you some more if—'

Gripping him by the shoulders, Peter pulled him off. Monika, free from Martin's grasp, began crying as the twins stood facing each other, their eyes filled with mutual indignation. Peter had never before stood up to his brother and wasn't sure what to do next – but, committed, he knew he couldn't turn away. The shock of pain was sudden; he hadn't even seen Martin move. But the ballooning sensation on his upper lip, the redness on his fingers was all too real. He hadn't fallen but his knees buckled. Martin stood poised a few feet away, his fists clenched and suspended, ready to strike again.

Behind his brother's shoulder, Peter caught sight of Monika, her hand clamped over her mouth, her eyes wide with shock. In the distance, they heard a voice, the woman's voice coming from the lake, calling out Monika's name. 'I'll get you back for this, Martin Fischbacher,' she said quietly. Composing herself, she ran her fingers through her hair, 'Coming, Helene,' she cried out in return. Peter caught her eye and for a moment felt hypnotised by their sea-green intensity. For years to come, he would speculate on that look, on that split second, and wonder whether her expression was one of empathy, or of disdain.

The twins watched her run away, back through the trees, towards the lake.

When Martin looked at him, there was no mistaking his scorn. With his bag slung over his shoulder, Martin shrugged, turned on his heel and marched off towards home.

'Martin,' Peter called out. 'Wait for me.'

'Sod off.'

'Martin, I didn't mean to…' But his brother was already disappearing into the trees. The leaves rustled. Peter wondered whether to try to catch up with his brother but decided to leave him alone. He'd be OK by the time he got back to the village. A cluster of white butterflies fluttered by. He ran his finger along his stinging lip and wished Martin hadn't stormed off before they'd concocted a story to present to their father. How quickly the woman in the lake had become an inconsequential memory. Instead, his mind was filled with Monika's expression; and, in his heart, a sorrow that his actions had caused Martin to hit him.

As he wandered home slowly, he pondered how he would ever make it up to his brother.

Chapter 2: Sisters

Monika took her shoes off and padded into the cold water of the lake. She was still shaking slightly from her altercation with Martin.

'Going for a swim?' asked her sister as she did her buttons.

'No, just wanted to cool down a bit.'

'It'll cool you down all right – it's icy. Lovely though.'

'Mama said we had to hurry.'

Helene rubbed her towel through her hair, her head cocked to one side. 'OK, let's go then.'

Helene walked ahead briskly, as she always did, and Monika had to trot to keep up. 'Those twins were here,' she said. 'They were watching you.'

'I know. I saw them.'

'Didn't you mind?'

'No, they're only boys.'

'Shouldn't we tell Mama?'

'You can if you want to.'

She fully intended to. 'One pushed me against a tree.'

'Really? Why did he do that?' Helene asked, sweeping away strands of wet hair from her face.

'Because I said I was going to tell on them.'

'So he pushed you against a tree? You poor girl.'

'Yes. And he was going to hit me but his brother stepped in.'

'Oh. In that case, you should tell mother. Nasty boys.'

They walked for a while in silence. Helene with her towel flung over her shoulder, surged ahead, the sun shining through her yellow blouse. The village came into view.

'They come from Berlin,' said Monika, running to catch up.

'I know that.'

'I want to live in Berlin one day.'

'What's wrong with here? Don't you like it with us?'

Monika knew her sister was teasing but still, she answered carefully. 'Of course, and I would come back all the time but think, Helene, think of all that excitement – the dance halls and the theatres and all those shops.'

'Only any good if you can afford to go in them. You'd have to get a job.'

'I will. I want to be a dancer.'

Helene laughed.

'What's so funny about that?'

'Oh, Monika, I'm sorry. I didn't mean to laugh. If you want to be a dancer, you go ahead, go to Berlin. Become a dancer.'

As they walked down through the village, they saw Mr Fischbacher. 'That's the twins' father,' said Monika.

'I know. He's going to the café.'

'Should we tell him – you know, about the boys spying on you?'

'God, no. Don't talk to him; he looks horrible.'

Chapter 3: The Bottle

Having returned from his daily pointless trip to the café, Adolphus eyed the bottle on the top shelf. It sat there, a quarter full, tempting him with its clear liquid. He could taste it, feel the joyous burning sensation as it cascaded down his throat. Everyday he fought this battle; everyday he lost it. Annoyed with himself, Adolphus spun away and flung himself onto the chair, desperately trying to delay the inevitable. He hadn't realized how much he was sweating. God, he wanted that drink – it'd make him feel better – and… worse. A lot worse.

He wished the twins would come back. Their presence, irritating as it was, took his mind off things, made him feel as if he was part of the present. Marta, his wife, would be ages yet. She'd got a job earning a degrading wage with Höch, a local farmer and Nazi-lover, the smarmy git. If only the communists had power – they'd have confiscated Höch's farm in the spirit of collectivization by now. That'd have taken the grin off his face. Pitiful though they were, Marta's wages were a godsend but how it hurt, how he resented it – to be dependent on her income, to have to feel grateful for every scrap. How he hated this life – this prison of a hut with its primitive clay floor and rotting wood, this fucking squalid little village with its inbred inhabitants, suspicious and simple. He knew they were all Nazi accomplices, gleefully handing over their Jews, happy to wipe the shit off their boots. He grabbed for his cigarettes, his hand shaking as he lit one, the pale blue smoke dancing in the rays of fading sunlight. If only he could go back.

The knock on the door was so quiet, he thought he'd imagined it. The second time, he realized he hadn't. No one had ever knocked on their door before, no neighbours, no friends (for he had none), and for a few moments he felt that overly familiar surge of fear that they were coming for him – but then the Gestapo aren't known for knocking gently. 'Come in,' he said, hesitantly.

The door opened noisily and a woman's face peeked round.

'Mrs Emmerich?' She didn't come in, as if unwilling to commit herself to his hospitality. Monika's mother was the only villager willing to bid him good day, and he accepted her greetings like a man starved. 'Well, come in, come in,' he said, conscious that his parched voice sounded like a growl. He cleared his throat. 'I won't bite,' he added, trying to sound more congenial.

She took a step in but remained at the door, her hands behind her back. A pretty thing, he thought, past her best but still attractive with her black hair tied in a bun and her green eyes. Her presence there, the way she looked at him, reminded him how unclean he was. But with no water beyond the dribbling tap at the back of the hut, what could he do, and the clothes he wore were his only set.

'Am I disturbing you?' she asked.

'No, not at all.' He stubbed out the cigarette, grinding it into an ashtray. 'Would you like a coffee?'

'No, I won't keep you long but I thought I ought to let you know…'

'Yes?'

'It's a little awkward.'

'Take a seat, Mrs Emmerich, take a seat. Is it the twins?'

She sat down on a wooden chair, her hands neatly resting on her lap. 'Yes, it's the twins. You see, I have two daughters, as you probably know. And the eldest, Helene, she likes to go swimming out in the lake in the woods.'

'The lake. Yes, I know it.'

'Well, I sent Monika out yesterday morning to fetch Helene – she'd forgotten an appointment we had and, well… Oh dear, I'm going to sound like an awful sneak. The fact is, Monika found your boys spying.'

'Well, they'll make good Nazi informants, then. Spying on what exactly?'

'They were spying on Helene, my daughter. In the lake.'

'Is that so bad?'

'Well, yes, because Helene was not wearing any clothes. She was naked.'

'Oh.' The accusation hit him as if he himself had been caught. 'The dirty little…' He felt a flush of shame as he sat down heavily. 'I'm sorry. I'll speak to them. Severely.' The dirty little bastards; he hadn't brought them up to behave like perverts. Had his father caught him spying on naked women, he would have received a well-

16

deserved hiding. Well, the twins couldn't expect anything different. It wasn't so much what they done but the fear that if it got round the village, they'd be labelled as degenerates as well as aliens. Fuck, what an existence, what a way to live. It never used to be like this. He needed that drink.

'Are you OK, Mr Fischbacher?'

He sighed. 'Yes, I'm OK.'

'Have you settled in now?' Her voice seemed laced with concern.

'Yes. No. I don't know.'

'What is it you used to do? Before you came here?'

'Me?' No one in the village had ever asked him before. 'I had a business a long time ago, importing and selling cloth from the US. I made a decent living. Good quality material was always in demand, especially in Berlin.'

'And then the came depression.'

'Yes, and then the came the depression. Then after that I became a communist; you probably know that. It's why I'm here. Exiled.'

'Could have been worse.'

'Yes.'

'You survived.'

'Yes, we survived. We were among the lucky ones.' He hadn't been that lucky – they arrested him and sent to one of the new concentration camps just opening. But he couldn't tell her that. The beatings, the degradation still hurt. He lit another cigarette. Released after a couple of months, and in that he had been lucky, he had his home confiscated and told to get out of Berlin. The following day they found themselves, with a suitcase each, on a train heading east, to this place that time forgot.

'You can't go back?'

'Of course not. I'm banned from travelling further than five kilometres from the village centre. It's part of the punishment – for being a *communist*.' He rubbed his eyes. 'Well, now you know my story. As a good German, you should hate me.'

'Not at all. Your wife, I see, has a job, and the twins seem to have settled in.'

'Except when they're being peeping toms.'

'Oh, I wish I'd never mentioned it now. It was Helene's fault. What was she thinking of, swimming naked? I'll speak to her. Well, Mr Fischbacher, it's been very nice but I have to get going now.'

But Adolphus was lost deep in thought, the cigarette burning between his fingers. When, finally, he looked up, she'd gone. Pity, he thought, she was nice. It'd been the first conversation he'd had in this godforsaken place. But instead of making him feel better, it'd only served to remind him how futile his situation was.

'I don't want a drink,' he muttered, his fingernails scraping against the wooden table. 'I don't want a drink.' The hours stretched ahead of him, hours of loneliness and boredom, hours of agony. He couldn't face it, he couldn't continue sitting there, pacing up and down this filthy hut, his memories full of happier, more prosperous times. He slammed the table with his palm. Stubbing out the cigarette, he rose clumsily from the chair, knocking it sideways, and lurched towards the shelves, reaching up for the bottle. Lunging at it, he knocked it and, for a moment, it tottered, threatening to fall, before settling back into place. Breathing a sigh of relief, he snatched it, uncorked the top and let the haze of fumes reach into his nostrils, launching a stream of saliva. With trembling fingers, he gripped the bottle and gulped down the liquid, feeling the burning pleasure as it slipped down his throat. He took in a heavy breath and held it there; savouring the moment, conscious of the tears prickling his eyes, such was his relief. As he breathed out, he smiled and felt his muscles relax.

'No more than a few sips,' he said, as he took a second swig, swiftly followed by a third. No, it never used to be like this.

Chapter 4: Liars

The thing about Martin, thought Peter, was that he took offence easily but equally he soon forgot. The day after the incident at the lake, they had walked the four kilometres to school in the neighbouring village as normal, his brother reminiscing about their life in the city. It was the same route taken by Monika but she always maintained a respectable distance and this morning, Peter noticed, she was nowhere to be seen.

Coming back from school, Peter felt pleased with the day – he had taken part in a dress rehearsal ahead of the school play, a rendition of *Little Red Riding Hood*. The teacher, Miss Hoffman, had given him the role of a tree and he was enjoying dressing up in green and waving branches around. He never mentioned it to his brother – Martin had been assigned a minor backstage role and although he would never admit it, Peter knew it rankled. But as they entered the village along the dusty road that ran through it, Martin brought it up. 'You know all your lines then?' he asked.

They cut through a cluster of chickens, causing a sudden whirl of feathers and flurry of squawks. The dirty little houses, all squat and rundown, never failed to depress Peter. 'I only have the one. You were there.'

'I wasn't really listening. I was planning.'

'Planning what?'

'You'll find out.'

Nearby, the bell of the village church pealed. A horse and cart receded into the distance. An old woman in a black shawl ambled by. Peter said good afternoon but received no response. The villagers had not accepted their presence yet.

Of all the squat houses, theirs was the worst. One floor and with just a couple of rooms, the low ceiling and tiny windows added to the feel of claustrophobia. Peter opened the heavy door, fearful of what sort of state his father might be in. Most days they found their father either asleep or in a vicious mood – both the result of drinking. Nervously, he stepped in, Martin behind him, his eyes adjusting to the dark.

The air stunk, as usual, of smoke, alcohol and sweat. On the table a bottle, empty, an upturned glass, and a newspaper that'd been there for over a week. And sitting on the floor with cigarette butts scattered round him, was their father, laughing quietly for no apparent reason. 'So, what the bloody hell were you two up to yesterday?' said their father, struggling to sit up.

The boys glanced at each other. 'Yesterday?'

'Yes, yesterday morning. Where were you?'

'Erm ... can't remember,' said Martin. 'Walking.'

Adolphus gripped a table leg and hauled himself to his feet. 'Where?'

'The forest.'

'Just walking, eh?' he said, taking a lolloping step towards Martin. 'Come across anything interesting?'

Martin stepped back. 'No.'

'You bloody liar, I know what you were doing, you dirty little sods.'

Damn her, thought Peter, Monika hadn't even hesitated.

'We were only walking, Papa, honestly. Weren't we, Peter?'

'Yes, Papa, out in the forest.'

Adolphus belched. 'Come across any lakes? Come on, answer me that, you peeping toms.' He lurched forward again, unsteady on his feet. 'I'll give you walking in the forest. I'll teach you to lie to me.'

'Stop it, Papa,' cried Peter.

'You're both a disgrace.'

'*We're* a disgrace?' shouted Martin.

Adolphus straightened, his face contorted in anger as the implication sunk in. 'Why you… you…'

'Leave him alone,' said Peter, surprising himself with the strength of his voice.

His father turned abruptly to face him, panting, spittle on his lips, fury in his eyes. Peter's stomach lurched. 'Papa, please,' he said, as his father's shadow fell over him.

Chapter 5: The Play

Standing on the stage behind the curtain, dressed as a tree in a brown checked shirt and a green cardigan, Peter peeked through the gap. The village hall was filling up as parents and friends took their places amid the babble of conversation. Monika joined him. 'Let's see,' she said. 'It's exciting, isn't it?'

'No. I'm terrified.'

'Listen to you. You'll be fine. Anyway, you've only got one line.'

'It's all right for you, you've done this sort of thing before.'

'Yes, I'm a natural, as they say. I can't see my parents yet.'

'I can see mine – right at the back.'

Monika scanned the audience. 'Oh yes. Ah, here come Mama and Papa – late as usual. I think the whole village is here.'

A voice called to them from the side of the stage. 'Peter, Monika, come back here.' It was Miss Hoffman, their teacher and, for these last few weeks, their director. The play, *Little Red Riding Hood*, had been weeks in the planning. Peter knew that the rehearsals, costumes and set design had taken all of Miss Hoffman's time. Monika had landed the lead part, and here she was dressed in a pink and white dress and a bright red cape. 'Monika, are you OK? All ready with your lines?'

'I'm fine, Miss Hoffman.'

'Good girl. And how about you, Mr Tree? Oh dear, where's your crown of leaves?'

'It's here, Miss H,' said Peter.

'Good. Don't call me Miss H. Now don't worry, you'll be great; both of you. Let's join the others.'

Peter liked Miss Hoffman; he liked the way her hair curled into her face, the smallness of her nose and her finely plucked eyebrows.

Behind the stage, a gaggle of schoolchildren tore up and down, some in costume, others trying to look authoritative. Miss Hoffman, carrying a clipboard, spoke to each one individually. Tomi, a short but tough boy with cropped hair, had landed the part playing the role of the huntsman, which meant a silly bushy beard and a large swastika sewn on the back of his costume, while his friend, Kurt, a tall, blond boy with a lazy eye, was playing the wolf, complete with a Star of David on his chest. Mr Manstein, the headmaster, a short, bald man with owl-like eyes, appeared, looking flustered and clutching a piece of paper. 'Everything ready, Miss Hoffman?'

'Yes, Headmaster. We're ready to go.'

'OK. Well, good luck to each and every one of you. Break a leg.'

'Break a leg?' asked a girl dressed vaguely as a tree.

24

'It's just an expression,' said Miss Hoffman. 'It means… oh, it doesn't matter now.'

Mr Manstein had taken his place on the stage in front of the curtain. The audience settled down. He welcomed the parents, waxed lyrical on the genius of the Brothers Grimm, writers of *Little Red Riding Hood*, and launched into a lecture on how great all German writers and composers and artists were.

Behind stage, Peter, now sporting his crown of leaves, and his fellow cast members listened, getting increasingly nervous. Miss Hoffman flittered around; adjusting hats, tucking in shirts, making sure her charges looked their best. As Mr Manstein finished his introduction, Miss Hoffman gave Martin a nod – his only task was to lift the needle onto the record.

As the music began and the opening bars sounded around the hall, the narrator, a boy called Albert, deemed to have the most authoritative intonation in the class on account his voice had broken, said his first lines into the microphone: "*Once upon a time, a long time ago, there was a young girl whom everyone called 'Little Red Riding Hood', because she never went anywhere without wearing a cap made of lovely red velvet that her grandmother had given to her…*" Monika took her place on the stage. The show had begun.

*

Backstage, ten minutes later, Peter was almost skipping with glee. The show was going down well, the audience had laughed in the right places and, most importantly, Peter had remembered his one line. Monika stood beside him waiting for her next entrance. 'This is fun, isn't it?' she said.

'Yes, but the strain of artistic endeavour is quite exhausting,' said Peter, adopting a pompous tone.

'Have you swallowed a dictionary?'

'I overheard Miss H saying it.'

'You are a fool sometimes, Peter. Oh, I'm next – better go.'

*

The show was nearing its end; Albert continued his narration: *"Our hero huntsman had climbed on a branch and had made a lasso with which to catch the Yid wolf…"*

Miss Hoffman hadn't been able to fashion a tree with an overhanging branch. Instead she had instructed a carpenter to build her a six-foot high wooden scaffold with a couple of rails. *"The huntsman was carefully lowering the lasso from the branch…"* Tomi, rope in hand, leant against the rail as the wolf circled beneath. With a loud and unexpected crack, the rail gave way. The audience gasped. Tomi crashed to the stage floor. Clutching his ankle, he let out an anguished cry. Some in the audience laughed, not knowing that Tomi's fall was not intended. Miss Hoffman pushed her clipboard against Peter's chest and ran onto the stage. 'Tomi, are you OK?'

'It's my ankle – it hurts,' he said between sobs.

The audience shuffled uneasily in their seats. A murmur of voices spread across the hall.

'That wasn't meant to happen, folks,' said Albert helpfully over the microphone.

Mr Manstein was also on the stage, feeling Tomi's ankle. 'OK, let's get you off,' he said. 'Miss Hoffman, tell someone to stop that ghastly music.'

'Martin,' she shouted. 'Stop the music.'

Peter, standing to the side of the stage, still sporting his leaves, turned to see his brother lifting the needle off the record. What he saw shocked him – Martin was laughing so much, tears were pouring down his face. Peter knew.

*

It was a girl in the year below that told on the twins. Later that afternoon, once the audience had dispersed and gone, and the children were preparing to go home, Mr Manstein called Martin and Peter in to see him.

He invited the twins to sit down. His office was bright with the sun streaming through the large window but it was small; enough room only for desk and a couple of chairs either side. On the desk, a pile of papers and folders, a fountain pen and a bust of Hilter, on the wall a large map of the world flanked by framed portraits of Hitler and the old Kaiser.

'The girl saw one of you Fischbachers with a hacksaw in your hand.' Peter felt himself wither as the Head held his gaze for a few moments with his owl-like eyes. 'So, you thought it'd be funny, did you, to saw the rail and then support it with tacks? Tomi is OK, no thanks to you, but he could have broken his ankle. So, was it you, Martin; or perhaps it was you, Peter?'

'It…'

'Yes?'

'It wasn't either of us, sir,' said Peter.

The headmaster steepled his fingers. 'This girl, who shall remain nameless, is an excellent pupil and I trust her implicitly. I appreciate she may have got you and your brother confused, after all, it's easy to do, but if she says she saw one of you with a hacksaw, I believe her. Which one of you was responsible for this act of sabotage? Which one of you saw fit to destroy Miss Hoffman's play?'

The boys glanced at each other. Go on, thought Peter, tell him, tell him the truth. But he knew, from his brother's determined expression, that he wasn't going to confess.

'It weren't me,' said Martin.

'Nor me,' added Peter with a sigh.

Mr Manstein narrowed his eyes. 'You have one last chance. Speak up or I shall have to cane both of you. Surely, whichever one of you it was, would want to spare your brother unwarranted punishment.' He spoke slowly – 'So, I ask again, which one of you was it?'

Peter's fingers tightened behind his back. If he ever needed his twin to be brave, this was it. He needed his brother to take responsibility for his own deeds. Surely Martin cared enough for him to save Peter from being caned. But as Martin kept his silence, the bitter truth hit him – his brother cared nothing for him. He had an idea – it was risky, but he needed to force the issue, to test his brother's loyalty. 'Headmaster, sir,' he said quietly.

'Yes, Peter?'

'It was me.'

Mr Manstein raised an eyebrow. For what seemed an age, he said nothing; Peter could sense his disappointment. Martin, not able to prevent himself, shot him a look. Finally, Mr Manstein spoke. 'Martin, have you anything to say?'

Please, thought Peter, say something. Prove yourself to me.

'Well?'

'Headmaster, sir, all I can say is that I am ashamed of my brother's behaviour.'

*

Half an hour later, Peter walked slowly home by himself, his hand down the back of his trousers, trying to ease the throbbing pain across his backside where the cane had done its brutal work. He was crying. But it wasn't the pain that was causing him to cry.

Chapter 6: The School

'OK, that's enough now, quieten down, please.' Mr Rich, the teacher, was wanting to start his lesson, dressed as always in his usual suit, an odd muddy brown colour and stained from excessive use, and his hair greased back, accentuating the carefully executed middle parting. Peter and Martin, as the sons of a known communist, sat towards the back away from the other pupils as if their mere presence might infect their loyal Hitler Youth classmates. The classroom was small but with enough desks and chairs to sit the twenty children in the class. Smudged-yellow paint peeled off the walls, the windows layered with years of grime, cobwebs hanging from the ceiling. Even on this warm June morning, it smelt dank, thought Peter, like an old man's vest.

Two rows in front of the twins sat Monika. She hadn't turned round to say hello as she normally did. Peter knew, without having to see her face, that she was still furious with him for having supposedly ruined the play. No one else knew – the Head had elected to keep it a secret. But Martin, compounding his malevolence, had told Monika. Thankfully, she'd kept it to herself. In turn, Peter still hadn't forgiven her since the incident at the lake. Would Monika have told on them if she realized what punishment they had to endure? But what had frightened Peter most was his father's hitting of their mother. Punished one day for working for a Nazi, punished the next for not earning enough; each beating a reflection of Father's own inadequacies.

But it wasn't his father's beating that had occupied Peter's mind but the expression on Monika's face after Martin had punched him in the forest. Peter had saved her from Martin's assault, taking the brunt of his anger. And each time he thought of it, he saw the look in her sea-green eyes, her hand clamped over her mouth, and hard as he might he could not decipher what the look meant. During his more fanciful moments, he saw himself as her brave knight, her eyes wide with admiration and gratitude. But now, instead, he knew she hated him for having sabotaged the rail. If only she knew.

As for Martin, the extent of his brother's baseness had left Peter reeling. His brother's betrayal had left him gaping in wonderment – he could not comprehend Martin's motivation and when he tried to reason it, his stomach tightened.

The morning's lesson was political studies, something that always made Peter feel anxious. His father's politics was not something he gave any thought to but he never felt so conscious of being the son of a commie as during Mr Rich's classes. He hated being labelled a communist, hated being reminded of it. He, himself, was not a communist – he wasn't entirely sure what it meant but, as he was often reminded, an apple never falls far from its tree. On the desk in front of him lay a school textbook on politics, containing chapters on the Social Democrats, the communists, Marxists and more. Flipping through the pages, Peter noticed the usual blank spaces – paragraphs and sections now politically out of favour hastily removed.

'Tomi, if you're quite ready.' Tomi, sitting on the far left of the class, leant back in his chair, his whole posture one of arrogance. Mr Rich raised an eyebrow as if thanking him for his ready obedience. Peter secretly admired Tomi. It was Tomi who had stuck the sticker on the blackboard that read: *Down with reactionary teachers* and none of the teachers had the nerve to remove it. He had suffered no long-term consequences of his fall. Next to Tomi sat Albert, the boy who had done the narration, a tall, good-looking fair boy, quite the perfect Aryan. The leader and his henchman. No teacher dared separate them.

Mr Rich cleared his throat. 'Right, today, children, we shall be following on from our discussion last week and asking how the Bolshevik swine managed to weedle their way into power in Russia…' An audible groan came from the left. Mr Rich tried to ignore it. 'And the events leading up to the so-called Russian Revolution. But first…' he paused for effect. 'I have to ask Martin and Peter to leave the room.' He grinned as he said it, pleased to have gained a degree of credibility with the children at the twins' expense. Peter felt the colour rise in his cheeks as the whole class (except Monika) turned to look at them.

'Martin? Peter, if you don't mind?'

Of course they minded but what choice did they have? Brothers together, communists together; a curse to be worn and endured thanks to their father. They rose and started gathering their papers. 'You can leave them there; you can come back after the break.'

Peter, closest to the door, led the way, Martin behind him. Peter kept his eyes fixed to the floor, not wanting to catch the sea of contemptuous grins as he made his way through the rows of desks. Someone threw a ball of paper, hitting Peter on the back of the head.

'Albert, stop that,' said the teacher with little conviction.

As Peter passed Monika, she coughed, a delicate, apologetic cough. Was it a coincidence or a signal?

The corridor was short. The whole school was small, a rectangular building with a corrugated roof, consisting of only five classrooms and a couple of offices. Each day, the twins walked the four kilometres to school, their rucksacks, containing books and lunch, strapped to their backs. Each day they arrived, tired, followed a minute or two later by Monika who walked the same path but kept a respectable distance behind them. The boys hated the hike while their parents envied their freedom to walk so far without question. Posters adorned the length of the corridor, proclaiming the National Socialist struggle, or the vitriolic lambasting of their enemies – Britain and France – the hated imperialists, or the dispicable, unpatriotic Jews. *Germany is a strong bastion in the camp of freedom; For us work is a matter of honour and glory.*

'We're going to have to do something about him, you know.'

'Who?' Peter had been idly staring out of the window, gazing over the walled compound of their school and across at the thatched roofs of the nearby village; a much nicer village than their own. An old peasant woman dressed in black trudged across the field, bent almost double. Old King Wenceslas came to mind.

'Father, of course, stupid.'

Peter knew whom Martin had meant. 'Like what?'

'I don't know, but we need to tame him before he kills Mother or one of us. We could denounce him in some way.'

'Denounce him? That would mean…'

'Exactly. We'd be safe.'

Peter hated it when Martin spoke like this, as if only he had the right to decide things; that Peter's own opinions counted for nothing. His only way out was to defeat his brother on a practical level, for once Martin had decided on something there was no shifting him from his belief that he was in the right. 'What would we denounce him for?' asked Peter, realising that by saying *we*, he was already allying himself with Martin's scheme.

Martin squinted, his mind turning over the possibilities, 'Tell them that he loves Stalin or something, or that he'd walked further than the four kilometres.'

'They notice if anyone breaks their curfew.'

'That he gets drunk and says anti-Nazi things. No one would doubt that.'

Peter felt the butterflies in his stomach. The peasant woman had disappeared from view. Martin was serious, he could see that, and perhaps what he said made sense, but he didn't like it. Yes, life with his father could be frightening; never knowing when the next beating may come, but he was still their father, and he couldn't imagine life without him.

'No, we can't.'

'Oh yes, we can.' Martin looked at him directly in the

eye. 'We must.'

'Not yet.'

'Why not?'

'He might get better, he might get a job, he might—'

'He might fly to the moon,' said Martin, throwing his arms up in the air. 'Grow up, Peter.'

Peter was desperately trying to think of another retort, when their classroom door swung open, and the first of their classmates appeared. 'You can go back in after break,' said one, as the group amassed in the corridor. 'He's finished now,' said another.

Peter was suddenly aware of Monika leaning against the corridor wall opposite him, her head lowered, her eyes peering out from under her fringe. His stomach lurched. Martin had started chatting to the group of boys. Peter wanted to say something to her, wanted her to say something to him. Instead, they stood silently opposite each other while others passed between them, a blur of featureless beings. Then a face blocked Peter's vision, the cropped hair, the aggressive eyes. It was Tomi.

'So, you bastard; you killed our Horst.' Behind him, stood Albert and others.

'I… I didn't kill anyone,' said Peter, stepping back. Tomi and his small gathering burst out into laughter, a threatening, accusing laugh.

'You're communists, aren't you?' said Albert.

'Yeah,' said Tomi. 'So you killed Horst Wessel, you Jew-lovers.'

'Fuck you, Tomi.' Martin had stepped forward where Peter had stepped back.

'You commies killed Horst Wessel.'

'And you peasant boys have got shit for brains—'

'What's going on here?' said a shrill female voice.

'Nothing, Miss Hoffman,' said Tomi.

'Well, what are you hanging round here for then? Get along.' The boys lingered a moment. 'Get along with you, I say. Martin, a word, please. You too, Peter.'

'It wasn't the twins' fault, Miss,' said Monika. Peter had forgotten about her and felt inexplicably pleased that she was still there. 'It was Tomi and the others. They were being rude.' Peter knew that it had taken courage for her to say the words.

'Were they indeed? No doubt whipped up by our good Mr Rich.'

'He said the commies—'

'Well, I expect Peter and Martin have heard worse in their time. Am I right?'

Martin looked at Peter, and Peter knew that faraway look, when his eyes drifted back through the years of their short lives. It was one of the few times when the brothers felt sibling affinity. They never spoke about it, not even to each other, and certainly not to a teacher, however sympathetic. But when Martin's expression drifted back to that uncertain past, it brought back for Peter that all-encompassing fear: the days with their mother waiting for Father to return from the concentration camp, fearful that they too, even as children, might get arrested, that they'd come for their mother. They were a family then. But a haunted one.

Miss Hoffman seemed embarrassed by their silence. 'Well, not to worry,' she said most quietly. 'We're safe with Hitler, our so-called saviour.'

Peter's heart quickened: her tone was insincere, the way she had emphasised *so-called*. He wasn't sure whether he had heard her correctly.

'One day,' she continued, lowering her voice, 'we'll be free of this tryanny. One day we'll be able to hold up our heads again.'

No one knew what to say; they didn't dare agree with her. It was Martin who broke the awkward silence. 'We… we ought to go, Miss Hoffman, we don't want to be late.'

'That's fine, off you go, and if you get any more trouble from Tomi and…' But Martin was already half way down the corridor. Miss Hoffman looked at Peter, who forced a weak smile.

'Thank you, Miss Hoffman,' he said, following his brother, Monika behind him. They had no desire to stay in the presence of a woman so loose with her words.

Chapter 7: The Head

The subdued morning light shone through the threadbare curtains. Peter stirred, opening his eyes, wiping away the sleep. Lying on her side, facing him, was his mother, the outline of her shape shrouded by the sheet, her face enveloped into the pillow. A strand of hair fell across her cheek. He lifted his head to see if Martin was still asleep the other side of her. But his brother had gone, the indent of his head still visible on the pillow. He was probably out, thought Peter, taking one of his early morning strolls.

Peter studied his mother's face – the length of her eyelashes, the delicate arc of her eyebrow, the definition in her cupid's bow, the faint hint of down on her upper lip. How it pained him to think that when she looked in the mirror, it wasn't these delicate features she saw but the all-too-recent scars of violence – the shadow of blackened red under her left eye, the swollen lip, the fading bruise on her cheekbone. How can a man do this to the woman he purports to love?

And sadly, things had gotten worse. His father had

made a friend, a village loner called Otto. Otto's presence in Adolphus's life had, at least, stopped his father's daytime drinking. Instead, Adolphus and Otto spent their days shooting the local wildlife in the nearby woods. But the evenings had become insufferable. The two of them went out drinking in the two village bars, returning to their respective homes inebriated. Each night, their father's imminent return caused the twins and their mother evenings of fearful anticipation, awaiting his obstreperous entrance and the violent language – or worse.

She opened her eyes and immediately focused on him. A drowsy smile spread across her lips. 'Hello, darling,' she said, her voice slow and husky. Her breath fell on his face, stale and sleepy, but it was his mother's smell and he breathed it in.

'School today?'

He nodded. She turned onto her back and stretched, her hands reaching back and touching the wall behind the bed. Yawning, she winced and her finger went to her lip and daubed the swollen wound.

'Does it hurt?' he asked.

'No.'

He knew she was lying, trying to protect him, as she always did. 'Why don't you leave him?'

'Oh, Peter, how can you ask that? He needs us – you, me and Martin. I can't just up and leave. Anyway, where would we go? We couldn't really lose ourselves in a village this small.'

'Mama, you're always making excuses for him, but he shouldn't be doing these things to you – to us. It's worse now with this... this man Otto.'

She sighed and turned to face him, with a look in her

eye and the knotted eyebrows that told him she was about to launch into something earnest. 'I know you won't ever forget what we went through when they took your father away, Peter, but you don't realise the full extent of how he suffered. Everyday, they used to beat him. But he was brave – he never let them beat him down. It was they, the camp, that made him what he is now.'

'I know all this, Mama.' If his father had been so brave back then, he wondered, why did he lack the courage now to admit that what he was doing to his family was so damn wrong. He could see the shame in his father's eyes when sober, as he waited for the headache to pass. Peter resolved never to show such weakness.

'Do you, Peter? Do you really know it? The Jews and us communists have suffered at the hands of Hitler and his party.'

'Our saviour; our so-called saviour,' interrupted Peter, thinking of Miss Hoffman.

'So-called? Peter, don't ever use that expression. No, look at me, look at me. Promise me, don't ever use that expression.'

'But…' He thought about telling her about Miss Hoffman but decided against it.

'Promise me.'

'They think we killed Horst Wessel.'

'He was nothing more than a Nazi thug. So, who said that?'

'The kids at school – they think we commies killed him.'

'But you must know they didn't banish us out here for that–'

'It was because of Papa's beliefs, yes, I know. And

now he's bitter and so he hits you and he hits us and you think you have this fantastic reason to forgive him every time he does it.'

He expected her to react angrily but instead her face fell deeper into the pillow. Her arm stretched out and lay gently on his shoulder. 'Yes, Peter, I do.'

*

On their hike to school, Martin talked further of denouncing their father, of 'ridding the family of its cancer.' Peter thought of his mother and her loyalty to her husband, and tried to work out whether her loyalty was misguided or heroic. But he said nothing.

He turned round to see Monika following them only yards behind. Each day, she seemed to be closing in on them. He wanted to invite her to walk alongside them but, as always, allowed himself to be swayed by his prediction of Martin's reaction.

As soon as they arrived at school, the twins realized that something unusual was happening – the teachers seemed agitated, the atmosphere tense. But when they asked round, none of the children knew why and the teachers weren't saying.

They had to wait until mid-morning before they found out. The first lesson had been German literature with Miss Kretschmann, a dreadful old widow who lectured with such a shrill voice, Peter always came away from her lessons with a headache. It was rumoured her husband had committed suicide. Having to listen to a voice like that every day, Peter didn't blame him.

Mr Rich took the second lesson, pulling nervously on his tie. His hair was so carefully parted, it made Peter think of a straight road running through a forest. The children settled down quickly hoping that Mr Rich would enlighten them as to why everything seemed out of the ordinary. They weren't disappointed – what he said was both satisfying and intriguing at the same time. Mr Manstein, the headmaster, said Mr Rich, needed to speak to every child in the school – individually. When their name was called, they should report directly to his office, and when finished, come back to class. They were not permitted to speak to anyone about their conversation with the Head, and the severest of punishments would be meted out to those who were caught gossiping. Almost as soon as he'd finished, Miss Kippenberger, sometime teacher, sometime Headmaster's secretary, knocked on the classroom door and entered without waiting for a reply. 'Tomi Schücking,' she said, without acknowledging the teacher.

Tomi looked at Mr Rich, waiting for permission to leave – an unusual show of obedience, thought Peter. 'Well go on, then, boy. Off you go.'

Tomi rose from his desk and grinned at the rest of the class, but Peter could see the uncertainty under the bluster. He saw it because he was feeling it too. What on earth could Mr Manstein want with all of them? And to see each of them, one at a time, was unprecedented.

Pulling again on his tie, Mr Rich launched into his lesson – the perfidiousness of Stalin on his route to power. He spoke in a low, rambling voice, his nerves on display, rendering it almost impossible to listen or take in what he was saying.

'And there he reamins to this day – enscouned in the Kremlin, surrounded by sycophants.'

After only a few minutes, Tomi returned; swinging

open the classroom door, his shoulders swaggering with arrogance, because he'd been through it and come back unscathed – whatever 'it' was. His eyes gleamed with satisfaction of knowing that he was in on the secret and no one else in the class so far, possibly including Mr Rich, knew what it was.

'It's Peter's turn,' he said, without addressing Mr Rich.

'OK, Peter – off you go.'

Peter went to tidy his books and papers.

'Go on then, boy, don't dilly-dally.'

*

The Headmaster began. 'A situation has arisen, young Fischbacher, that needs the utmost integrity and honesty. I expect you to be frank with me and not to hide away any facts that may be of assistance. I expect you, also, to put aside any feelings of personal loyalty and to remember the country is, and must always remain, your first priority. Any other loyalties are irrelevant. Do you understand?'

'Yes, sir.'

'It has come to my attention, Martin, that a serious allegation has been made against one of the teachers in the school.'

Peter squirmed, reluctant to interrupt. He coughed, lightly, 'Headmaster, sir–'

'Yes, yes, what is it?'

'I'm Peter, not Martin.'

The Head glanced down at his notes and then peered at Peter, as if trying to spot the difference between the twins. 'Yes, of course – Peter.' He cleared his throat. 'The teacher concerned is Miss Hoffman. The allegation against her is that of anti-Party agitation.' The Head paused for effect and Peter accordingly absorbed the revelation, his face reddening. 'Miss Hoffman is, without doubt, a popular teacher but I must reiterate that her crime is as such that any misguided loyalty must be put to one side.' Peter noticed the subtle switch from allegation to presumed guilt. 'Our political system and our survival as a nation state under the glorious National Socialist system is still very much in its infancy. Like a flower, we need to nurture and protect it against the slightest digression from the rightful path. So, Peter, with this in mind, I have to ask you, what evidence can you provide me of Miss Hoffman's political deviation?'

We're safe now with our so-called saviour. His heart had skipped at her use of the phrase, uttered so casually, as if these dangerous words were but random, innocent words. Who had heard her say them? Martin, Monika and himself. Could someone else have overheard? Had she repeated them, or something similar, elsewhere? Was she in the habit of saying such dangerous things?

'Well?'

Peter liked her, always had done; she had a heart, a personality, she stuck out from the other teachers for her individuality; and now she was being made to pay for it, for her lack of conformity. He didn't care what Mr Manstein had said, she'd saved him from a beating and for that he'd always appreciate her. But what if Martin or Monika told Mr Manstein the truth? Then the Head would know of Peter's concealment. The humiliation of taking the blame and the beating following his brother's prank at the play still rankled.

'For pity's sake, boy, do you think I have all day? You

know something; what is it?'

'No, Headmaster, I don't; I was just trying to remember.'

The Head leant forward, as if trying to see into his eyes. 'Are you absolutely sure? I warn you, Fischbacher, you cannot afford to lie.'

'I know, Headmaster, but it's true.'

'So, you have never heard Miss Hoffman utter or pronounce anything that could be construed as anti-Party?'

'No, Headmaster.'

'OK.' Satisfied, the Head leant back in his chair and picked-up a sheet of paper from a pile on his desk. 'Sign this and then you may go back to class.' He pushed the paper across the desk, and pointed at a fountain pen.

Peter read the short typewritten document:

I, the undersigned, petition that Miss Hoffman *should be tried and punished with the strongest possible sentence for* anti-National Socialist agitation. *No leniency should be afforded to the above named.*

Long live Germany.
Long live our Führer.,
Signed

....

Peter's hand shook as he scanned the words. Her fate was already as good as sealed. He looked up and was confronted by the Head's face leering down at him. 'Well, aren't you going to sign it?'

He couldn't possibly sign it, and equally he knew he couldn't possibly *not* sign it. His hand reached out for the fountain pen.

45

Chapter 8: The Announcement

Dear Führer, how we love you; o, so merciful and wise. Our Führer, how we adore you; o, so gracious and kind. Martin and Peter were singing heartily, as was the whole school, some one hundred pupils and their teachers standing to attention in the school's walled courtyard, basked in sun. It was one of the few times the children could yell at the top of their lungs without fear of a clip or a whack. Following the ode to the merciful and wise Führer, the children sung the Horst Wessel song and various odes to the party. If he leant forward and peered to his left, Peter could just about see Monika, her hair tied back with a red ribbon that matched her kerchief.

'Thank you, children,' said Mr Manstein. He waited for the children to settle, casting his paternal, owl-like eyes over the gathering, their white shirts reflecting under the bright sunshine. 'We shall take our pledges.' Peter could feel the silent, collective groan. 'Put your right hand over your heart and repeat after me… Dear Beloved Führer, please listen to my pledge to you, devoted and true.'

Dear Beloved Führer, please listen to my pledge to you, devoted and true…

'I vow to you, beloved and wise leader, to the great Reich that we proudly call our own… that I dedicate my life, my learning and my future… and for the sake of National Socialism and freedom I shall not stray from the rightful path …'

I shall not stray from the rightful path …

Peter leant forward again, his hand against his chest. This time, he caught Monika's eye and the flicker of her smile.

More pledges followed, Mr Manstein's diction clear and upright, echoing across the courtyard; the children's response, one hundred dulled voices, sweltering under the heat. Relieved to sit down, Peter hoped for the chance to sing again, simply to help him shake off his heavy head and clear his foggy mind.

'OK,' said the Head'. 'You may sit.'

'We already are,' muttered Martin under his breath.

'Today, I have a grave and unpleasant announcement to make,' bellowed Mr Manstein. The one sentence was enough to re-focus the children's attention.

'Here goes,' whispered Martin.

'As you will be aware by now, we have discovered a malicious critic of our national leadership in our midst. Fortunately, the keen ears of one of our most devoted students has put paid to her scandalous gossip. It upsets me personally that this person is a member of my staff. As adults in charge of children, we are beholden with a responsibility to your education, to your welfare and your future. Equally, I am relieved and indeed grateful that without exception every child in this school voluntarily signed the petition demanding the application of the severest punishment suitable for a case of this kind. Miss Hoffman has been relieved of her duties and will soon be placed at the mercy of the authorities who shall decide on her fate. Let us hope they take into consideration our signatures. And let us hope she serves her sentence with dignity, reflecting on the error of her ways and that she relishes the opportunity to repent. Miss Hoffman, you may be surprised to learn, is still with us. On her behalf, I have asked the authorities to allow Miss Hoffman the opportunity to speak to you today. You may remain seated and I expect total silence.' He paused for a few moments. Rarely, thought Peter, had Mr Manstein gained the children's unswerving attention. 'Miss Hoffman, if you please…'

Her appearance shocked Peter and the pupils. The once immaculate and attractive Miss Hoffman now looked dishevelled, her face stripped of make-up, her eyes puffed-up. She stood in front of the children, some of whom hissed at her, her eyes desperate, gazing heavenward, wringing her hands. How small she seemed now, the fallen idol, naked without her authority, drowning in a rising crescendo of hissing. Peter hoped Mr Manstein would step in and reclaim the silence he'd demanded. But the Head seemed content to stand to the side, allowing his former teacher to experience the school's derision.

'Children… my, my dear children.' Her voice, quiet and hesitant, shook, its very vulnerability shocking the children into silence. 'I have been very foolish and I have rightly earned the disrespect of my colleagues – my *former* colleagues – and, more sadly for me, of you, my wonderful pupils.' Now, she looked directly at her silent audience, carefully scanning their faces as she spoke, her words slow and deliberate. 'I am guilty of everything you've heard today. I am no better than a common traitor or a spy. I will stand later today in front of the Gestapo and I shall accept whatever charges they place before me and I shall accept whatever punishment comes my way. You were right to sign those petitions, each and every one of you.'

She continued, her voice quivering on each syllable. 'I want to… to apologise. I have shown you a bad example. You must forget me, forget I ever existed. But I, I shall never forget you, my dear, dear children. I shall remember you all – your happy faces and your happy smiles. I will never…' She tried to speak again, but her words were smothered in tears. 'I will never forget you, children.'

She turned and fled, her hand at her mouth, and ran into the darkness of the school. The children watched her disappear before realising Mr Manstein was ready to address them again.

Peter had tears in his eyes and, as he looked at his fellow students, he realized he wasn't alone; they were all united in weeping. The hissing had been part of the game, the pantomime of booing the bad guy. But when faced with the real thing, they knew the meaning of victimisation and scapegoating, even if the words were still alien to them. They were crying for all the Miss Hoffmans of Germany, the missing relatives, the disappeared parents, the forgotten friends; they cried for the uncertainty of her future and the uncertainty of their own. They may have all signed the petition with their hands but none had signed with their hearts.

Sensing their mood, Mr Manstein seemed momentarily uncertain, faced with a sea of unspoken sympathy for the so-called traitor who had dared to speak of the so-called saviour, who had dared to put into words what many believed, students and staff alike. 'We, er… We trust that our collective petition has the desired effect. We shall now have our community lecture of the day – no, perhaps not yet. I think, instead, we'll have some more singing.'

And Peter knew why – the Head knew that any lecture now would only give the children chance to ponder on Miss Hoffman's speech and cause resentment to stir within their young hearts; better to break the spell with some active participation.

*

The three of them walked home together – Martin, Peter and Monika. Peter wondered how and at what point Monika had so subtly ingratiated herself into their routine; a shift of status that neither he nor Martin had noticed until her everyday presence was already accepted without question.

They ambled home for the most part in sullen silence, each still coming to terms with their pity for Miss Hoffman's plight. The wheat fields shone in the white heat, a crow squawked, the countryside droned with the hectic sound of insects.

As they approached the edge of the forest, Martin broke the silence. 'OK, who sneaked on her?'

Monika and Peter looked at each other, surprised by Martin's assumption. 'What do you mean by that?' asked Peter.

Martin stopped walking. 'It's obvious, isn't it? Only us three heard her say so-called saviour, no one else. So, one of *us three* went running to Manstein and sneaked on her. And it bloody well wasn't me.'

'And it wasn't me either,' said Monika.

Martin and Monika looked at Peter, 'Well?'

'Nor me.'

'So, that makes one of us a liar as well as a sneak.'

'Don't be silly,' said Monika. 'She could have said it, and worse, dozens of times to lots of different people.'

'Funny then that she's exposed the very day after she said it to us.'

'Doesn't mean anything.'

'You're very quiet, Brother.'

'So what – that makes me guilty, does it?'

'Well, you speak like one who has something to hide.'

'Hello, boys!' Their father's greeting came from behind them. They turned to see him emerging from the forest, about thirty metres away, carrying a bulging leather bag. The boys waved. Following their father out from the trees came a plump man with a rifle. This, thought Peter, was probably Papa's new companion.

Their father caught them up, his cheeks flushed, a smile on his face. 'Coming home from school?' he asked cheerfully, dropping the leather bag on the path. 'Hello, Monika.'

'Hello, Mr Fischbacher.'

'Otto, come meet my boys.'

Otto, with his rifle cocked and slung over his shoulder, strolled bow-legged up the path. He wore a large cap and gumboots that reached over his knees. One of his eyes, his left, reflected the sun and looked odd, thought Peter. 'Hello there, your father's told me all about you,' he said, the movement of his lips lost beneath a huge

51

thickness of beard.

'Oh, right.'

'Oi, Martin, more respect for my friend.'

'Ah, I have a boy just like him.'

Yes, thought Peter, but do you beat him every time you come home drunk. Instead, he asked politely, 'Shoot anything, Papa?'

'I'd say he did,' interrupted Otto. 'For a beginner, he's one hell of a shot. I reckon he's done it before. Shot a few Yids in your time, eh, Adolphus?' Peter couldn't help but wonder if there was something wrong with his eye.

'Look in here, boys,' said his father. 'A pheasant and two rabbits, we'll eat like kings tonight!'

Monika recoiled at the sight of the twisted mass of dead animals, but Peter was impressed. Even Martin raised an eyebrow. This was rare occurrence, thought Peter; his father had earned some degree of respect.

'And then, Otto,' continued Adolphus, 'we'll paint the town red, eh, what d'you say?'

'By town, you mean our shithole of a village?'

The two of them laughed; Adolphus's arm round Otto's shoulder.

The twins looked knowingly at each other and imperceptibly shook their heads. The thought of their father returning home late, drunk and violent, filled them with dread.

Chapter 9: The Hunt

Adolphus felt hung-over but then he did most mornings. But he was damned if a thumping head and a queasy stomach was going to stop him from making the most of Otto's rifle. Sunday was his friend's day at the market in the neighbouring village, four kilometres away. The evening before, in a drunken show of friendship, he'd agreed to let Adolphus use the rifle for the day. And Adolphus felt honoured by Otto's trust, for Otto said he'd never lent it out before.

Adolphus enjoyed his evenings with his new friend. After months of despair in this godforfuckingsaken village in the land the Nazis forgot, it was a relief to have found a mate, for here, in this shithole, time dragged. Generally, things had slowly started improving – the villagers were gradually coming round to accepting the exiled commie and his family. His wife, Marta, and he were now on civil speaking terms with the neighbours, as were the twins with their daughter, Monika. And then Otto appeared. What a man with his glass eye, his rifle, and his capacity for drink that rivalled his own.

Marta prepared his breakfast – porridge and coffee, standing at the stove, wooden spoon in hand, a fresh bruise on her face. The twins sat at the table with him, neither of them saying much, sullen as usual. He knew why, they didn't like him hitting their mother; they resented it. Wimps. His own father used to dole out far worse to him and his mother, and did he complain? Did she? No, of course not, wouldn't dare to, but it did him, and her, a lot of good, taught him to be tough, to be a man. It prepared him for life.

'So then, boys, ready to come out later with your old man?'

Silence.

'Martin? Peter?'

Still silence.

'Well, what about it? I'll teach you how to fire the rifle and who knows, you might bag your own supper.'

'Do you really think that's wise, Adolphus?' said Marta from the stove.

'Oh, for goodness sake, course it is.'

'But a rifle? You forget sometimes, they're only thirteen.'

'If they're going to become country boys they might as well start learning to live like ones.'

'I'm not happy–'

'I'm not asking whether you're happy with it, they're coming out with me and that's it.'

He caught a flicker of a smile on Martin's face and felt vindicated. He reached out, placed his hand on the boy's arm and winked at him.

*

The forest felt cool after the warmth and effort of trekking through the wheat fields. With Otto's rifle cocked and slung over his shoulder, Adolphus felt rejuvenated – the hangover was gone, his stomach full, his lungs full of country air.

'Come on, boys, keep up.' They caught him up, panting. They were enjoying themselves; they wouldn't admit it but he could tell, especially Martin. They shared half a bottle of water between them. 'We've got a kilometre or two to walk first, and then we'll see what's around. OK?'

'Yeah, sure,' said one.

'OK,' said the other.

'Good lads; let's go then.'

They should do this more often, he thought, it did him good to make time for his sons; did them good to spend time with their old man. They were good lads really. It couldn't have been easy for them, used to city life, to be thrown out here. Strange to relate, he was beginning to enjoy the simple life, divorced from the worries over the welfare of the working classes, the suppressed and the exploited. When he looked back on it, he couldn't have cared less for them.

Everything was simpler here, his needs more basic – shooting, drinking and the occasional fuck – what else did a man need? And now that he was thinking about it, that little girl's mother was rather nice. Fulsome breasts and that seductive smile. He hadn't taken much notice of her that time she came to tell him of the twins' peeping tom activities but that was back during his darkest days. The girl, Monika, she had her mother's looks. One day, she'd make a good wife for one of the twins. Assuming she could tell one from the other. Maybe, the boys could take turns with her! She'd never know the difference.

They'd reached the spot Otto always gravitated to. A good place for rabbits and birds. Otto told him he once shot a kingfisher at the lake, which, considering their size, was no mean feat. Even if it was true, which he didn't think it was, Adolphus hadn't approved – didn't seem right shooting something so beautiful.

'Right then, boys, keep your voices down,' he said quietly, even though they had hardly said a word all morning. 'If we lie down for a while in this shallow bit, we might get lucky.'

The twins sat cross-legged in the indent, and looked as if they were expecting a picnic. 'No, no, not like that; flat – on your stomachs. That's it.' He squeezed in between them and lay with his chest on the lip of the hollow, the rifle pointing out. 'Now, keep quiet and something's bound to come along soon enough.'

The forest hummed with unseen activity – squawks, squeaks and shrills; an abundance of wildlife but, as yet, none of it visible. Time seemed to tick by and, conversely, stand still at the same time. But either way, it didn't matter – time was the one thing he had plenty of now. He turned round and Peter had dozed off next to him. A nudge in the ribs brought him round. 'Sorry, Papa,' the boy mouthed.

Adolphus smiled; this was, indeed, the life.

'Shush, I saw something move,' he said. He clicked the safety catch off the rifle and lowered his eye to level the sight. 'It's a rabbit. There, look. See it? Come on, my beauty, a bit closer… that's it, stay still for Papa Adolphus, keep still, my darling, keep still…'

The crack of the shot brought an eruption of sound throughout the forest, a community of wildlife scurrying, flapping, darting. Behind him, the twins held their breaths.

'Yes! I think I got it – quickly, boys, let's see.' He clambered out of the hollow, the twins on his heels skipping, the three of them whooping with excitement. 'Over there,' he said, running, pointing.

He was acutely conscious of his foot slamming into the tree root, the loss of balance, his arms sprawling, hitting the forest floor, and then the explosive crack of a gunshot. A boy's scream pierced the air, screeching up into the trees that suddenly seemed taller than ever.

Chapter 10: Call For Help

Adolphus and Martin stood stock still, their mouths gaping open in shock, the rifle on the forest floor where Adolphus had dropped it. Peter lay on the ground on his side, his hands clenched round his thigh, the blood pouring out between his splayed fingers; his leg trembling. His face, already deathly white, contorted in pain.

Adolphus and Martin looked at each other, each mirroring the other's fear, their eyes searching for the answers to questions impossible to formulate. Peter's mouth began emitting a strange noise, strangulated and desperate. Adolphus screamed, falling to the ground over his son. 'Peter, Peter. Oh, God, help me.'

Martin suddenly jerked into action, pulling his shirt off over his head.

'What're you doing?' asked his father, his voice thin, shaky.

'A bandage.' But Martin realized he had a problem – how to prise his brother's hands off his thigh long enough to apply the tourniquet. 'Papa, help me,' he shrieked.

Adolphus tried to pull away the iron-gripped fingers one by one, his own fingers quickly becoming submersed in blood as his son's guttural noises increased. 'I can't do it.'

'We must.'

'You bloody try, then.'

Martin attempted to pull the hands off by the wrist. The blood, sticky and warm, was coming in torrents. The howl of pain took him by surprise, his brother's mouth wide open; screaming so loudly Martin thought the forest would cave in. The leg was now visibly shaking, a pool of blood coagulating on the dried leaves. Adolphus knew his own resolve was weakening, his heart pumping so wildly it drowned out his thoughts. Peter's screams seemed to be penetrating into his brain until he felt as if the noise was coming from within him. How he wanted to escape, to dissolve into the forest and pretend he'd never been there, that this was someone else's nightmare and not his own. 'He's going to bleed to death,' he shouted. 'It's too far to run; I don't know what to do.'

'We have to try,' said Martin, his eyes full of tears. 'I'll go.'

'Go then, boy, go.'

Peter had stopped screaming, instead emitting a constant groan while his father crumpled into a fit of sobs. Peter's thigh was now soaked in blood, his reddened hands stuck fast over the hastily-bandaged wound. Then, Peter opened his eyes and looked straight at him. 'Papa, please…' he muttered, before closing his eyes and screeching again.

'Get going, boy!'

Martin never realized he could run so fast. The trees

passed him in a blur, his feet barely touching the forest floor. He ran down a slope that gradually steeped. By the time he reached the bottom, his feet couldn't keep up with themselves and he fell and slid through a carpet of leaves. Bracing himself for the pain that never came, he sat up, his breath loud enough to block out all other sounds except that of his heart. He wiped his brow and realized his whole body was soaked in sweat. I've got to keep going, I've got to keep going.

He still had a good kilometre back through the wheat fields to get to the village, the shithole, as his father called it. Unable to run at speed any more, he jogged, conscious of the noise in his chest; of his heart weighing him down.

The ramshackle village was in sight now – the whitewashed one-storey houses with their sun-baked thatched roofs. In the distance he could hear a dog barking and the drone of the village's one tractor. His legs felt as if they were made of wood, he couldn't catch his breath. The scene in the forest came back to him – Papa's face as white as chalk, the pool of crimson red, the quaking leg, the faint smell of cordite. He picked up speed as he approached the village, rehearsing a scrabble of words, wondering whether to break the news to his mother.

He decided to head straight for the more popular of the village's two cafés. It was Sunday lunchtime and, as he expected, every seat outside was occupied. Nowadays, at least, he could approach people without them whispering "Here comes one of the commie boys". His face was familiar to them now.

'Excuse me,' he said, his head still pounding, conscious of the sweat pouring off him. 'Excuse me…' He feared he was about to faint.

Gathered round a wooden table sat about five men, each with a glass of beer, and a tray of nuts between them. 'My, what have we here?' said one of them, a village elder with a long beard, wearing his Sunday best. 'Are you all right, lad?'

Trying to control his breathing, Peter pointed towards the forest. 'My brother. He's been... been shot.'

'Shot?' said the men in unison.

'What do you mean shot; are you sure?'

'Accident. The rifle. He's shot.'

'Otto's rifle?'

Did it matter whose bloody rifle it was? 'Help him... please.'

The elder spoke for him, taking charge of the situation. 'Well, don't just sit there like lemons, you idiots, go help him. Hans, you requisition Mr Wittmann's car – we can drive round the back way; it'll be quicker. Max, you grab Dr Reger from his Sunday shag; Matthias, you get to Butcher Schmidt and take one his meat trolleys – we might need it as a stretcher; and Wilhelm, you get me another glass of beer.'

The man called Hans spoke. 'Mr Wittmann won't let us use his car on a Sunday.'

'Silly old fool. Tell him I said it's a party order; that should sort him out. Get to it then, you idiots.'

Martin watched as the motley specimen of villagers each took a last swig of their drinks and only then, reluctantly, took up their orders. Hans shot him a grudging look. Martin realized how much they'd resented having their Sunday routine interrupted. None of them looked as if they were in any urgent hurry. He felt grateful that someone had taken control and relieved him of the responsibility. 'Thank you, sir.'

'That's all right, lad. Once a soldier, always a soldier. Now, how did it happen?'

Martin skimmed through the events, his breathing still too laboured to allow him to relate the details.

The elder nodded knowingly as if it was a daily occurrence. 'What about your mother? Does she know yet?'

It was only then that the thought hit home – he might never see his brother again. By the time they reached his brother, he'd probably be dead. The full impact of this thought took a few seconds to absorb. And as the notion exploded in his brain, he burst into tears.

PART TWO:

**Three years later,
Hitler's 50th birthday, 20th April 1939**

Chapter 11: Birthday

'And so, on this tumultuous day, fifty years ago, Easter Day 1889, our great leader was born.' The speaker, Michael Zeiss, the squat-faced chairman of the local Nazi Party branch, had been speaking for over a quarter of an hour and Peter was bored. 'Never before has a country been in such need, never before had this proud nation of ours called out in such desperation. Hyperinflation, economic ruin, the cruel legacy of the war, the repressive terms of the Versailles Treaty. All that humiliation, a stain on our proud history, wiped away by the genius of one single man. Adolf Hitler, the greatest friend this country has ever had, the greatest political and military leader of all time...'

It was Hitler's fiftieth birthday. The day had been declared a national holiday; the country celebrated. War may have been on the horizon but today, at least, was to be a day of national celebration. Zeiss proposed a round of three cheers for 'our beloved Führer.' Dotted round the fringes of the audience were various hard-looking men in uniform, men of the Gestapo, there to ensure the villagers enjoyed themselves in a sufficiently appropriate manner.

The communities of the three local villages had gathered for the birthday celebrations. Chairman Zeiss delivered his speech from a two-foot-high podium, erected specifically for the purpose by Peter's father's glass-eyed friend, Otto. Every building, every house in the village was decked in swastika flags and banners, the villagers all wore their best outfits and greeted each other with hearty 'Heil Hitlers' and handshakes and kisses.

'Hip, hip, hooray…'

'Hooray…' Peter, clad in his Hitler Youth uniform, cast his eye over the gathering, two hundred or so villagers. Old men with fulsome whiskers and pipes, younger men in dungarees, specially ironed, women with floral dresses and ribbons in their hair, elderly matriarchs in black, wrapped in their best shawls, Party members in their uniforms and Nazi armbands. Two hundred hoorays, two hundred smiles but only a handful of happy hearts amongst them. Except perhaps his own – for eight days ago, Monika had returned. A sick aunt in Lübeck had taken Monika and her mother away almost a year ago. Finally, the aunt had died and now they were back. And what a difference a year makes. The shy girl of eleven months ago was now a self-assured, self-aware young woman of sixteen. Her hair had cultivated an attractive wave, she was taller, elegant and, what's more, she'd grown a bust, fantastic breasts he couldn't help but admire. Both Martin and he had fallen over themselves when they first clapped eyes on her, refusing at first to believe this stunning girl was the same Monika they'd always known and reluctantly tolerated.

Problem was, every other boy in the village had seen her, and now the boys from the neighbouring villages as well.

'And now,' announced Zeiss, 'the schoolchildren will sing for us…'

One could hear the collective groan. What a relief to be sixteen, thought Peter, because the choir included every child aged fifteen and under. Last year, at the Heroes' Memorial Day, he too had sung *The Rotten Bones Are Trembling* and the *Horst Wessel Song*: "The flag on high! The ranks tightly closed!" But now, he could stand and watch with the men and the older boys of the village. He folded his arms and breathed in. *No more a child am I.*

Chairman Zeiss made his way off the swastika-bedecked podium and suddenly, with a shriek, half disappeared from view. A burst of laughter broke forth from the crowd. Peter craned his neck – Zeiss's foot had gone through a plank of wood on the podium, and he was now being helped out by two ashen-faced village elders. Otto, who'd been standing not that far from Peter, vanished. Zeiss re-emerged, red-faced and dishevelled, his glasses skewed across his nose. 'Who's responsible for this contraption?' he bellowed, as the laughter died away, the crowd conscious of the steely Gestapo men watching them with narrowed eyes.

'Really sorry, Chairman, perhaps it wasn't assembled properly,' said one of the elders.

'Why in the hell not?'

Another elder whispered in Zeiss's ear. That's Otto done for, thought Peter.

The children sung robustly, their words crisp and rehearsed because, as Peter knew, they would have practised the songs numerous times daily for weeks on end, so that they'd all be heartily sick of them by now.

He could see Monika speaking to Tomi and Albert, also in uniform. Tomi, once the class rebel, had seen his status gradually diminish as his weight rapidly increased while Albert had grown unfeasibly tall. Monika looked bored by them both, her eyes darting this way and that, looking for an escape. By God, she was lovely now, and she knew it. What a change, what a transformation. But a small part of him missed the Monika of old, the Monika he could speak to without blushing, the Monika he could ignore but was always there. Their happy gang – Martin, Peter and Monika. But now she was too much a catch to be considered automatically theirs – every boy wanted Monika for himself. Including Tomi. Poor old Tomi, with his boy breasts and his flabby eyes – he was wasting his breath on her. But Albert, tall, blonde and handsome… well, he was a worry.

'I know what you're thinking.' Martin had re-appeared.

'No you don't, you don't always know what I'm thinking.'

'I reckon it's fairly obvious in this instance,' he said, nodding towards Monika.

Peter rolled his eyes. 'Fair point, I suppose.'

'She's going to the dance. I'm asking her out.'

Peter was appalled, having had the same idea. 'You can't.'

Martin laughed. 'And pray, why not?'

'Because…'

'Oh, don't tell me, because you, my dear brother, were planning the same.'

There were, thought Peter, distinct drawbacks in having telepathic minds. 'Maybe.'

'Well, may the best man win and all that, but you can't dance with that leg of yours.'

'Can.'

'Nah, and I'll tell you now – you may as well give in.'

Typical Martin, thought Peter. 'Why should I?'

'Because,' said Martin, lowering his voice, 'I have a secret weapon guaranteed to melt any heart.'

Peter knew by the flash in his brother's eyes that this was not bluff. 'What? Go on, tell me.'

Martin laughed again and tapped his nose. 'See you later,' he said, as he slid away into the crowd.

Mercifully, the children had finished their recital, concluding with a rousing ode to the Führer and his achievements. The gathering clapped politely. The Gestapo men clapped in an exaggerated, almost comical fashion, a direct signal to the assembled that their applause lacked sufficient enthusiasm. The crowd accordingly took their cue.

So what, wondered Peter, was this secret weapon of his brother's? He headed home, determined to discover, because whatever Martin was hiding, it was bound to be in the house somewhere. His father was standing outside, near the front door, smoking. 'Hello, son. You OK?'

'Fine thanks, Papa.'

His mother was inside, entertaining a couple of her female friends. A pan of water boiled on the stove. 'Tea, Peter?'

'No thanks.' He headed straight for the boys' bedroom. Even at midday, the room was dark with only the feeblest of light bulbs to cast any light. He delved under Martin's bed, ran his hand behind the books, checked through his clothes, looked inside his boots – but nothing.

Perhaps it was just a bluff after all; Martin playing psychological games – he wouldn't put it passed him. He was determined, for once in his life, not to play second fiddle to his brother. But somehow, he knew fate would be against him – as always.

*

The day passed with more speeches that no one dared miss, more singing, and even a parade. The younger children snaked through the village dressed as fat Jews, stamping their feet and singing *The Stars and Stripes* with ironic passion. How proudly they wore their grotesque masks, with pillows stuffed down their shirts, and bearing banners with slogans writ large: *Let their blood run on our swords, the time of the Jew is over!* The villagers greeted them with much laughter and applause.

Then, in the corner of his eye, he saw Martin with Monika. The two of them were giggling and sharing a joke. Immediately, Peter lost interest in the parade and felt the bitter taste of jealousy rise up within him. As the procession snaked along, the adults followed, stamping their feet in time with the children's singing. He noticed Martin and Monika join the procession somewhere in the middle. Peter followed suit, ten yards or so behind, and found himself next to Tomi.

'Fun this, don't you think?' said Tomi, his chin wobbling. 'That Monika turned out tasty.'

Tasty? What a revolting word, thought Peter. How dare he pass opinion on her; she'd been part of his gang, it was too late for the likes of Tomi to try to muscle in. He wanted to lay some sort of claim on her but realised that unless he acted quickly, Martin alone would steal her for himself – secret weapon or no secret weapon. The parade was now marching down the main street that divided the village into two. And then he saw them go, a quick sprint towards the café and behind.

He hesitated for a moment, wondering whether it would be unseemly to follow them.

'You know what,' said Tomi, 'Monika promised me a dance tonight.'

To think, thought Peter, I used to fear you, even respect you. But the thought of him pressing his corpulent self against Monika was too much. 'Excuse me, I've got to go.'

'Hey, Peter…'

But Peter was gone.

He ran soft-foot towards the café, round the back and almost ran straight into a gathering of Hitler Youth uniforms. Martin and Monika and Albert and another youth Peter didn't recognise were all standing in silence, looking at each other.

'Peter,' said Monika.

'Oh, hi.'

'Well,' said Albert, shuffling from one foot to another. 'We'd better be off.'

'Yeah,' said Martin. 'You do that.'

They watched Albert and his friend saunter off. Albert threw them a glance over his shoulder.

'What was that about?' asked Peter.

Monika giggled, her hand over her mouth. 'You wouldn't believe it, we found them–'

'Doesn't matter,' barked Martin.

'What you doing here?'

'Doesn't matter,' repeated Martin.

'Go on,' said Monika. 'Let him have some.'

Martin sighed; whatever it was, he was obviously reluctant to share it. 'If I must. Here we are,' he said, passing a bottle to his brother.

'What is it?' The bottle had a long thin neck and a red label with foreign writing; the liquid inside was jet black.

'Try it.'

He took a gulp, the black liquid, slightly warm, trickled down his throat, the bubbles bursting on his tongue – it was fantastic; he'd never tasted anything like it. 'Wow,' was all he could say.

'Good, isn't it?'

'Yeah.' He took another mouthful.

'That's enough, that's the only bottle I've got.'

'What is it?' he asked again, passing it back.

'It's Coca-Cola,' said Martin, triumphantly.

Coca-Cola. Even the name was tinged with danger. He wanted to ask Martin how he'd got hold of it but decided against it. Nazi propaganda had denounced the stuff as America's opium for the masses. Being caught with it could bring no end of trouble. So this, he thought, was what the American youth drank. Lucky them; it tasted like freedom.

'It's lovely, isn't it?' said Monika.

'Quick! Someone's coming,' said Peter.

The sound of shuffling boots became louder as they approached. It was Otto, his face red and puffed, his blind eye closed.

'What happened to your glass eye?' asked Martin, straight to the point.

'Bastards nicked it.'

'Why would they want to do that?'

'Because that stupid beggar, Zeiss, put his foot through my scaffold and I get the blame. They've taken my eye and won't give it back until I've fixed it.' He dabbed a stained handkerchief to his lip. 'Bloody Gestapo,' he added, as he traipsed off.

*

The dance began as the evening drew in, the final attraction on Hitler's birthday celebrations. Lanterns tottered on the end of long poles, a large tarpaulin had been draped on the ground for the dancers, a few children sat on bales of straw round the edge and, to one side, sat the band – four elderly men with banjo, violin, guitar and penny whistle. While the band played popular country songs and traditional folk tunes, the villagers gathered round the dancing area, with glasses of vodka or jugs of beer in their hands, and urged each other to dance before being forced into it by the men in uniform. At least, tonight, they'd be spared the Nazi anthems. Children scrambled between the grown-ups, sliding through legs, darting across the tarpaulin. A stall had been set up, providing refreshments and, nearby, a bonfire blazed, the matriarchs of the three villages sitting round the flames, sizzling sausages on toasting forks and handing them out.

Further afield, a number of entertainments had been set up for the villagers to try their hands at – pillow fighting on a raised log, tightrope walking, juggling and knife throwing. Not surprisingly, no woman would ever volunteer to stand against the board while drunken villagers threw knives at her; instead, the men had to make do with sacks stuffed with straw, made to look vaguely human-shaped. Some bright spark had stuck two semi-inflated balloons to the middle sack to represent breasts.

Martin, Monika and Peter were sprawled on the ground, propped up against a couple of straw bales, drinking beer and watching two sturdy young peasants wearing checked shirts hit each other with pillows on the log. 'I promised Tomi a dance tonight,' said Monika, casually, a twin either side of her.

'What on earth did you do that for?' asked Martin.

'I couldn't get rid of him. He's changed while I've been away.'

Martin laughed. 'Ever since his parents had to be re-educated in the meaning of being true National Socialists.'

'Arrested?'

'No, just duffed up a bit. Y'know, shown the error of their ways. Anyway, changed Tomi; turned overnight into a model Hitler Youth.'

Peter closed his eyes and breathed in the night air, the bonfire fumes and the smell of burning sausages. It was rare to feel so content; how happy he felt to be here, lying next to Monika, feeling her warmth. 'Here's to the Führer,' he said, raising his jug. 'May he rule wisely over us.'

'Here's to Otto, more like,' said Martin. Otto had been their supplier of beer and for Monika, a vodka.

One of the check-shirted boys lost his balance. A few more blows from his rival and he was off. The winner raised his fists and the onlookers cheered.

'Why don't you two have a go,' suggested Monika.

'Don't think so,' said Peter.

'Chicken.'

The check-shirted boys shook hands and, with arms round each other, staggered back towards the bonfire.

Monika peered at her empty glass. 'Whoever wins may take my hand for a dance.'

'You're only saying that to save yourself from Tomi.'

'Take it or leave it.'

'I know,' said Peter. 'How about a tightrope contest, instead.'

'With your leg? I'm game if you are,' said Martin, rising to his feet. 'Not so physical. I'm too drunk to do physical.'

'The winner may—'

'Yeah, yeah, we get the idea.'

Suspended about two feet from the ground, the rope stretched taut for about ten feet between two solid iron poles, each pole positioned next to wooden platforms. 'Did Otto make this?' asked Martin, stepping onto the fragile-looking contraption.

'Of course,' said the portly chap in charge of the rope, as he handed Martin a balancing baton made of three bamboo sticks tied together.

Martin stood on top of the ladder and removed his shoes, throwing them in Peter's direction.

Peter could smell Monika's presence next to him in the fading light. 'What do you think?' she said quietly.

'He won't stand a chance.'

'I hope not.'

It took him a few seconds to register her meaning and when he had, the whole world suddenly seemed a better place.

Martin had barely gone three steps when he began to falter. Another step or two and then he came crashing off, falling with exaggerated drama. 'It's harder than it looks,' he said, picking himself up and passing the baton to his brother.

Removing his shoes, Peter knew he couldn't help but win. Monika wanted him to, what greater motivation could there be? Six steps to win, that was all, six small steps.

The rope may have been thick, but Martin was right – it was damn difficult. A haze of bonfire smoke drifted over him, the smell of burnt toast filled his nostrils. He tottered and jerked one way then the other, but with the fourth and then fifth step secure, he gained confidence, his body adjusting to the precariousness of the rope. Six, seven steps, he could walk forever, Monika was his for the night. Eight, nine and finally ten steps before his left heel slipped and he found himself on the ground, his legs straddling the rope. 'Champion,' he called out, raising the baton into the air. A few steps on a rope had beaten Martin's secret weapon, his bottle of Coca-Cola.

*

The dance, fifteen minutes later, proved to be awkward. Not enough people were dancing, too many watching, including Martin, Tomi, and Albert and his friend. Otto was there too, now sporting an eye-patch. Peter didn't know where to put his hands, felt unsure when to move left or right, or forward or back, unsure of the rhythm, which seemed to change subtly every so often. He laughed heartily, trying to disguise his embarrassment; Monika laughed with him but he never felt such a fool and he began to regret winning her hand. The crowd clapped to the music, occasionally losing time. After what seemed an eternity, it finally finished. Mightily relieved, Peter took an exaggerated bow, while Monika responded in kind with a curtsy.

As he led her away by the hand, he caught sight of Tomi's grinning face. 'My turn next,' said Tomi, his cheeks dimpling.

'Not tonight, Josephine,' said Peter firmly, leading Monika away from Tomi, away from his brother, but exactly where to, he wasn't entirely sure.

They carried on walking, giggling occasionally. By the time they stopped, they were behind a small cluster of isolated trees, about two hundred yards away from the western side of the village. With the light of the bonfire and the lanterns, Peter hadn't realised how full the moon was.

'Well,' said Monika. 'Now that you've brought me here, what are you going to do with me?'

Had he hesitated, even for a moment, he wouldn't have done it. He pushed her gently against the tree trunk and kissed her solidly on the mouth. But something was wrong – he was trying too hard. Like the dance, it felt awkward but this wasn't something he could brush aside with an embarrassed laugh. She shoved him away, causing him to feel ashamed. He forced himself to look at her, and he noticed the reflection of the moon in her eyes. Then, most gently, she took his hand and placed it delicately on her breast before pulling him forward and kissing him.

This time it felt perfect.

PART THREE:

**Six years later,
February 1945, Berlin**

Chapter 12: The Cellar

There were so many people crammed together, perhaps a hundred, thought Peter. Packed in, no one could move. The sense of claustrophobia had been heightened by the low ceiling, the grey-painted walls and the sandbags covering every window. The murmur of voices remained constant, occasionally punctuated by a shout of complaint or plea. 'That's my foot, you fool.' 'Friedrich? Where's my Friedrich?' The cellar stunk of oil from the flickering lamps, stale air and sweat, squashed down, it seemed, by the ceiling. Peter tried turning his head but couldn't escape the foul breath of onions coming from Mr Mann's mouth, a grizzled and bearded gentleman that lived on the floor above, or the drenched armpits of his older friend and downstairs neighbour, Oskar, all six foot-something of him with his long face and sunken cheeks. The elderly folk were dotted round the sides, sitting on the few available chairs. One of them, an elderly man with half-moon glasses, read his book, the epitome of calmness. Peter could see Monika but, having been separated, couldn't get to her. She smiled weakly at him. They'd been asleep when the siren sounded. Quickly but still in a sleepy haze, they'd donned their dressing gowns and joined the mass exodus of weary residents heading towards the basement, the stairway becoming more congested with each descending floor. Time had no meaning down here in the basement. Peter could overhear people complaining about the lack of sleep, about having to get up at five in order to catch the train to work. He knew the feeling but for once he and Monika were off the hook – tomorrow was Sunday. 'Don't worry,' shouted Jünger, the block warden, from the far end near the door. 'We're safe as houses down here.'

'Not the best analogy, you idiot,' came an immediate response.

'Who said that?'

Oskar guffawed to himself – 'Safe as houses, ha, ha.'

They could hear the firing of the flak, the anti-aircraft guns. 'Go get them!' shouted Jünger.

People, many also in dressing gowns, tried not to shake their heads. To be seen openly disagreeing with Jünger could be interpreted as defeatism but the flak seemed so puny compared to the British bombs that everyone knew was coming next. Sure enough, moments later came the sound of massive explosions. 'Still a long way off,' mouthed Oskar.

But not for long, thought Peter.

He could feel the tension rising in the cellar as people braced themselves for the onslaught. A young girl, no more than sixteen was crying, trying not to, failing to stifle her tears; a woman with a headscarf, perhaps her mother, her face red with sweat, crossed herself; another, holding onto a baby wrapped in a blanket, tightened her hold on her infant. Her husband, behind her, his hands on her shoulders, leant down and whispered something in her ear. Words of encouragement, she forced her lips into a smile. The sound of bombs came closer; the young girl's crying became louder. 'Stop that,' said the familiar voice of Mrs Rudel, the block's most ardent Nazi, nauseatingly proud her husband, a major, no less, fighting on the Eastern Front for *us* and the Fatherland. Mrs Rudel – well over forty, never seen without a swastika pendant on her lapel, never seen without the brightest red lipstick, never known to have uttered a pleasant word unless it was about the Führer and the Party. 'There's nothing to worry about,' she continued. 'It'll be over before you know it.'

Reinforced, maybe, but the cellar still shook as the bombs fell above them, plaster fell, clouds of dust, lights flickered. Instinctively, everyone ducked while covering their ears.

'God preserve us,' came a voice nearby. People swore, shook their fists at the ceiling, some cried. The baby started howling. The mother, kissing its head, tried to calm it.

'Can't you shut that brat up?'

The father spun round, trying to find the owner of the voice.

More bombs fell.

'How many more months will we have to suffer this?' asked Mrs Busch quietly, the baker's widow who lived across the hall from Peter and Monika.

Mrs Rudel heard her. Shouting to be heard above the continual rumble outside, she shouted, 'The time will come, don't you worry about that. We'll get our own back. The Führer knows what he's doing.'

Oskar nudged Peter in the ribs. 'Just wish he'd hurry up and get on with it then.'

'What was that, Oskar?' said Mrs Rudel.

'Eh? I was just saying to Peter here, we have absolute faith that the Führer will see us right.'

Peter wiped his brow of sweat, God it was hot. His leg began to throb as often it did when he'd been on his feet too long.

'Stupid cow,' said Oskar, lowering his voice. 'They say the Russians are already passed the Oder.'

'Really? That means they could here any week.'

'Have you heard what they've doing in Prussia? They fuck any woman they see – the old, the young, the deformed. They don't care – they're raping our woman, Peter. You think this is bad, wait until the Ivans are here. Then we'll pay for it, especially the women.'

The room shuddered, a cloud of plaster and dust fell from the ceiling. A couple of women screamed.

'That was a big 'un,' said Oskar.

'Monika,' cried Peter. 'You OK?'

She nodded, her face streaked with dirt, glistening with sweat.

No one spoke, listening, waiting for the next bomb. The minutes ticked by.

'I think I'm going to faint,' said Mrs Busch.

'Not much longer,' said Mrs Rudel.

Sure enough, as if on cue, the bombs stopped. An uneasy silence fell, waiting for the all-clear. People began to speak in hushed tones, as if fearing anything louder would attract the planes back. 'Are you sure?' said Peter, pushing up to Oskar. 'What you said about the Russians.'

'Your girlfriend over there – she's a pretty one.

Whatever you do, son, get her out of here. Go west; throw yourselves at the mercy of the Yanks, anything.'

'They won't let us travel without passes.'

'I know that but people do, don't they? Where there's a will…'

'I wouldn't know who to ask.'

'Find a way; do what you have to do. Just get her out of here before the Ivans arrive. I'm telling you now.'

The welcome sound of the all-clear was greeted by a cheer. Jünger pushed his way through, jangling his keys, the aura of self-importance following him, and opened the reinforced doors. The blast of cold air swept in. The relief. It was over – for at least another few hours or, if they were very lucky, another whole day or two.

Chapter 13: The Prodigal Return

Peter and his brother had returned to the city as seventeen-year olds in the spring of '40, six months after the war had broken out. While German troops were asserting the nation's right over the Poles, the twins settled down to enjoy the delights of city life. Their mother remained in the village, accustomed to rural life and her more subdued husband. The shooting accident may have tamed their father, as Martin had wanted, but the twins didn't miss him, not for an instant. They had hugged each other as they re-entered the city of their birth. As brothers, they'd never been closer as they soaked up the thrill of urban life. Doomsayers predicted that bombs would fall on the city, but no, they'd be safe – Hermann Goring had given his assurance, and that was good enough for them. "If one enemy bomb falls on Germany," the head of the Luftwaffe had said, "you can call me Meyer." Two months later, Monika joined them and started a course on dance, far more glamorous than their own engineering courses. Peter was elated to welcome her back into his arms while aware that at the same time, something disappeared in his new-found relationship with his brother.

And together they shared an apartment in a down-to-heel suburb in the eastern part of the city. Things were going well – too well. They knew it couldn't last, their lives were simply too frivolous at a time of war. Sure enough, four years ago, the summer of '40, the twins received their call-up papers, ordering them to report at the recruiting battalion headquarters at a specified time. They duly turned up, only for Peter to be sent home almost immediately. His father's shooting rifle had left him with a permanent limp. He returned home unsure whether to be relieved or ashamed. Monika's reaction didn't help. 'Surely, they could have found you something to do,' she'd said. Meanwhile, Martin passed his physical and mental examinations with ease – after all, a former Hitler Youth boy, he'd done his two years' conscription; he was a fit young man of 18; there'd be no reason for him not to. Monika's dancing school had closed down; now she worked as a teacher of primary school kids while Peter now worked as an assistant to the manager of a state-run munitions factory.

A bright autumnal Sunday morning, Peter and Oskar were returning home with a loaf of bread each and a few vegetables and a lemon – their fruits of having queued for hours. 'Chin-up,' said Oskar. 'Could be worse.'

Peter frowned. 'Don't see how.'

Oskar wore, as usual, his woolly hat with its earflaps tied over the head and a long burgundy-coloured coat. Like an urban scarecrow, his six-foot-five frame marked him out from the crowds milling about.

They made their way home through the wrecked streets, gazing vaguely at the now familiar sights of destruction – facades blasted away, lampposts bent, fallen timbers, trailing tramlines, broken glass littering the ground, fragments of brick and stone strewn around. Two elderly men sat on an upturned crate at the roadside, leaning on their walking sticks, their coats filthy and torn, their shoes caked in dust. Oskar laughed. 'Look at them,' he said. 'That'll be you and your brother in a few years' time.' Near them, a burnt out car, covered in soot.

Their apartment block on Kaiserstrasse had largely been spared the bombs – again. It always amazed Peter how it could survive such attacks, but apart from some damage to the roof, superficial stuff, Jünger had described it, it remained standing while neighbouring blocks had been pulverised.

Peter invited his friend in. Oskar declined, saying he had things to do.

'Like what exactly?' asked Peter.

'Sleep.'

Peter returned to an empty apartment and had a wash. The bath was full of water – a ready supply in case their water was cut off. Taking Oskar's lead, he lay on the settee and dozed off.

There was a loud knock on the apartment door. It wouldn't be Monika, who'd gone out to use her meat rations, she had her own key. Groggily, he rose to his feet, rubbing his left thigh, just above the knee, a constant reminder of the shooting accident. Another knock. 'Coming,' he shouted. How long he'd been asleep, he didn't know. It was not yet lunchtime, the sun, streaming through the shattered windows, exposed the layers of dust everywhere.

He went to open the door, fully expecting to see Mr Jünger who, as blockwarden, made not infrequent calls on all his tenants.

It took him a few moments to register – a soldier on his threshold, a great coat, a hefty rucksack over his shoulder, a finger hooked round the strap of a helmet knocking against his leg. His mind momentarily clouded. 'Is that–?'

'Hello, Peter.'

His heart thumped. That was his voice alright. 'Christ, I didn't recognise you.'

'Good to see you too,' he said quietly.

'My God, what… what are you doing here?'

'Aren't you going to invite me in?'

'What? Yes, yes, of course. C-come in.'

Peter stood at the door, his hand on its knob, watching as his brother traipsed into the apartment, dropping his helmet, letting his rucksack slip off his shoulder, yanking off his coat, leaving them all heaped on the floor, and almost falling onto the settee. 'Christ, I'm knackered. Any chance of some coffee?'

'Ersatz?'

'That'll do,' he muttered, his hand, on the side of the armchair, propping up his head.

Feeling suddenly self-conscious, aware of his brother's presence, Peter filled a pan with water and lit the gas. Waiting for the water to boil, he picked up his brothers things from the floor and hung them all on the coatrack. The coat, crusted with dried mud and dirt, felt heavy. It all stunk; even the rucksack stunk. Then, hoping his brother wouldn't notice, he washed his hands. Martin had aged; his eyes seemed almost lifeless, lacking in any expression except perhaps resignation and a deep weariness.

'I didn't think you'd still be here,' said Martin without looking up. 'I see the whole street's gone up in smoke. Whole fucking city has.'

'Are you on leave?' asked Peter, fearing it sounded more like an accusation than a question. He realised he hadn't seen his brother for over three years, not since the day in '42 when he left for the Eastern Front. A couple years before that, he and Monika had seen Martin off to France in his new uniform of the Wehrmacht.

'Yep, ten days. Ten whole days. Compassionate leave.' He scratched his head.

'For whom?'

'I told them my mother had died.'

Peter managed to stop himself from saying something.

'How's Monika?'

'Monika? She's fine; she should be back soon. Gone shopping.' How simple he made it sound – gone shopping as if it didn't involve hours of queuing, arguments, elbows and the constant risk of an aerial attack, and all for a couple half-rotten potatoes or some beans.

'Hmm, so she hasn't run off with someone else then.'

You bastard, thought Peter. 'So, how's Russia?' he asked.

'Very welcoming,' he said, scratching himself again.

'Really?' Too late he realised he'd fallen for his brother's idea of irony. 'I mean, what's it like compared to Paris?'

His brother laughed without feeling. 'Paris! Hell, that seems like a lifetime ago. Oh, Paris. It was like a holiday camp. Jesus, what I wouldn't give to go back there.' He shook his head, momentarily lost in the memory.

'Here's your coffee,' said Peter, placing it on the table next to the settee.

Martin grabbed his arm, holding him still as he was bent down. God, he stank, thought Peter, sweat, dirt, unwashed clothes. 'Papa did you a favour, shooting you. You know that now, don't you?'

'Yes.'

Martin let go, took a sip of his coffee. He didn't grimace at the taste of it; he'd probably had far worse, thought Peter. Closing his eyes, Martin leant back and very quickly fell asleep.

Peter sat at what Monika optimistically called the dining table and watched his brother. His face was heavily tanned but engraved with a deep fatigue, the first hints of grey were showing at his temples. In no time, his brother had fallen into a deep sleep, sprawled on the settee, his head thrown back, his mouth open. He looked weak, thought Peter – verging on skeletal, his fingers long and bony, his fingernails black with dirt. And inside – inside something had broken; that much was evident. War had changed him. It was obvious it would do – yet it still shocked Peter. Looking at him now, it occurred to him that he could go for days without giving his brother a single thought. He was happier without him but… but he was out there, fighting for the nation, seeing things Peter couldn't even begin to imagine. Peter knew it, had always known it from that day in 1940 at the recruiting station, that he felt deeply emasculated. Being rejected from that place, being sent home as unfit for service in any capacity, had been a defining moment. Ever since, he'd lived under the label of being weak, of not being a man when his nation needed men more than ever. But being at home, at the mercy of the bombs, was no picnic either, but it didn't count; at least he knew it wouldn't in the eyes of Martin. And no, Monika hadn't run off with someone else. They'd been together too long for that.

Ten days. He was back for ten days. It wasn't so long; it'd soon be gone. Unless, of course, the British hadn't blown them to smithereens by then.

Martin woke up. Rising unsteadily to his feet, he stretched his arms. The apartment door opened. A moment's hesitation then she screamed on seeing him. Dropping her bag, Monika flew across the room, flinging her arms round him, repeating his name, too excited even to notice the stench. Martin staggered back, laughing, trying to keep his balance, batting off a whole fusillade of questions. When did you get back, how long you're back for, why didn't you tell us, is it really you; God, we've missed you; we've been so worried about you. Haven't we, Peter?

Peter, reheating his brother's coffee in the pan, replied in the affirmative.

'I wrote to you, said I'd be back,' said Martin once Monika had calmed down.

'We didn't get it,' said Monika, sitting on the edge of her chair, leaning forward.

'The post has gone a bit dodgy,' added Peter.

'Let's celebrate,' said Monika. 'I got some eggs. I'll bake us a cake. We've got a lemon. You need feeding up, Martin. Look at you; there's nothing left of you.'

'I managed to get a few days leave and then I'm back. I never thought I'd find you. Have you heard from mum and dad? I never thought… never knew it'd be like this. It never stops. The fighting, I mean, the killing. The killing, it just… It's good to be back. Even if half the city is destroyed. Still good. God, Russia's fucking horrible. There's no end to it. You can walk for days. Days and days. You look at the map and realise you're still on the outline. And the Russians, they even send their women to fight. People call them subhuman. I thought that harsh at first but it's true – they bloody are, the whole lot of them – subhuman.' His eyes kept flicking round the room, unable to hold anyone's gaze for more than a second or two. 'This place, the flat, it's just as I remembered it to be. Bit dusty. We could do with a new carpet. And the doorbell – it needs fixing. I thought, once it's all over, I mean really over, we could go on holiday somewhere. Somewhere faraway. The States, perhaps. Imagine going there. Hollywood, Empire State. Full of Jews, they tell me, Jews and Negroes. Doesn't bother me. I'd go live on the moon with a bunch of fucking aliens if it meant not going back.'

'Is it really as bad as people are saying?' asked Monika.

'We keep hearing reports about the where the Russians are.'

Martin nodded. Peter and Monika watched him as he lit a cigarette. 'I don't know what you've been hearing but yeah, we're being pushed back at a rate of knots. We can't hold the front. I'm tired. I could sleep for a week.'

'What about these new weapons we keep hearing about, these wonder weapons?'

Staring into his mug of coffee, he said, 'Yeah, right. Wonder weapons. That should do it. You got anything to eat? Meat, soup, something like that?'

'Yes, we can find something. Martin, have you got lice? You keep scratching yourself.'

'Everyone gets lice.'

'We'll have to see to it. We've got some powder in the bathroom.'

During the course of the afternoon and the evening, Monika looked after him – running him a bath, helping him shave, washing his clothes while Peter, feeling redundant, wished he could simply vanish.

Chapter 14: Wounded City

The following day, with the sun out, the three of them went for a stroll amidst the ruins. Martin, wearing civilian clothing, said he wanted to see the damage for himself. Peter and Monika had to slow down, to allow Martin to keep up. Walking gently, they picked over the rubble and broken glass, Martin stopping frequently, gazing at the destruction, houses stripped of their facades, of buildings reduced to a pile of timber and bricks, of large, gaping craters, the red dust that never settled. Cars blackened and pulverized clogged up a street known for its wealthier apartments. Everywhere the stench of burning, of ash, of death. In one ground floor apartment, a woman was washing clothes in her sink, seemingly oblivious to the fact that her outer wall was no longer there. Martin stopped to watch people hurried along, their clothes and hair coated in dust, couples pushing their few remaining belongings on carts or wheelbarrows looking for somewhere new to sleep. At the bottom of one street, piled in a doorway, a pile of corpses, a mangle of twisted limbs and grotesque faces. Scooping down, Peter picked up a golden necklace. Martin stopped at a ripped poster on the ground, caught under half a brick – a painting of Hitler in profile, the words in bold gothic script, *The Führer will lead us to victory*. Further along, they watched a group of people using their bare hands to remove a small mountain of bricks, searching for survivors buried within.

They went to the park and together sat on a bench, the only one visible that hadn't been buckled or damaged in some way. Everywhere were trees uprooted, bent double. A couple of feral cats scavenged amongst the fallen branches. 'This is nice,' declared Martin, staring at the reflection of the sky on the lake that dominated the middle of the park. 'Where are the ducks?' he asked.

'Probably eaten,' said Monika.

Martin had bought a newspaper, *Der Stürmer*, and began reading aloud from it.

'Anyone would think we were playing a football tournament,' he said, flinging it to one side. 'It's all about attack and defence, regrouping, orderly retreats and victory is still ours to be had.' He paused. 'To think people believe this shit.'

A mother, dressed in a shabby coat, her hair greasy and unwashed, passed, pushing a pram. It was only as she got closer did Peter notice the yellow star.

'When will it all end, Martin?' asked Monika.

'If only I knew, Monika.' He shook his head. 'If only I knew.'

They stayed for an hour, maybe more. Martin, lying on the grass with the newspaper over his face, fell asleep.

Peter and Monika watched him for a while. 'He's changed, hasn't he?' said Monika quietly.

'Yes. I'm not sure how but he has.'

'I wonder what it's like out there.'

'In Russia? It can't be easy. He'll tell us when he's ready.'

'We ought to go soon. Find something to eat.'

'A few more minutes.'

Eventually, with the sun at its highest, they left the park.

'How you feeling, Martin?' asked Monika as they entered the desolate street that had once been the most-sought after in the vicinity; a thriving community of flats and shops and cinemas reduced to a wasteland. But still, people scurried about, anonymous identical figures searching for food or shelter or both.

'I don't know. Tired. Glad to be back, worried about having to go back. Hungry.'

'We'll look after you. Ah, there goes the siren.'

'Already?' said Peter. 'It's not even lunchtime yet.'

'Look.'

Following his brother's gaze, Peter's heart quickened on seeing the mass of planes in the distance – numerous V-shaped formations of English bombers filling the sky. 'My god, there must be hundreds of them, thousands.'

'Quickly, we need a shelter,' said Monika, her eyes scanning the street. People all around scattered in different directions, mothers screaming for their children, old women hitching up their skirts to run more quickly.

Their approach was swift, the hum of the engines intensifying with each second. If it wasn't so terrifying, thought Peter, the sight of the sun glinting off those metallic birds could almost be considered beautiful. An absurd thought.

'For God's sake, Martin, hurry up,' shrieked Monika.

'I can't go any faster.'

The hum had, all too rapidly, become a roar. Peter could hear the rattle of their machine guns, the whistle of falling bombs. The first wave swooped over them like a swarm of wasps, the noise deafening. Instinctively, they threw themselves onto the ground. Bullets pinged against brick and stone blowing up balls of dust. A house at the end of the street caved in on itself, victim to a direct hit.

Getting up, the three of them ran but where to, Peter, his mouth full of grime, had no idea. He clashed into someone, where they'd come from he didn't know. Spinning round, he realised he'd become separated from the others, unable to see through the clouds of smoke and dust. There was nowhere to hide. Some of these houses might have cellars, even the ones that lay in ruin, but he didn't have the time to seek. Frozen by indecision and abject fear, he called out for Monika.

More planes, their noise crushing him. Again, the rattle of machine gun fire; death from the skies. He'd fallen in a pothole behind a blackened car. Monika appeared behind him. 'Where's Martin?' he asked.

'I lost him.'

Taking her hand, he led her on; surely they'd find a shelter.

An elbow in the face caused Peter to spin round. A lad of the same age stared back, his eyes wide with fright. And then the boy fell into Peter's arms. Peter caught him. The boy was hot, covered in sweat. 'Peter!' screamed Monika. Peter let the boy go. The boy fell limp. Peter's hand reached again for Monika. They touched but her hand shot back on contact as if caught by an electric current. His hands were red, soaked in blood.

Sitting upright against a wall, a mother with her arms wrapped round her baby – a neat crimson hole in her forehead. It was the woman from the park – the Jewish mother.

Monika's face was contorted with pain. We're living our last few moments, thought Peter. I love you, Monika.

It was as if a hammer smashed into his teeth. He didn't see the person whose elbow caught him so fully on the jaw. He staggered. Falling to his feet, his fingers slipped away from hers. Monika turned. Her hands to her face, she screamed. Only an elbow, Monika. But the blood. Christ, the blood. Oh, fuck, he'd been hit. It felt strange, not quite real. He didn't know what had happened, the pain was there but it was the panic that overpowered him. He didn't know what to do. The helplessness of it. Help me, fuck, help me. What's happening, it was hurting like hell; he was fading away, the world so full of noise was suddenly and strangely very quiet. All these people, so close, so distant. He was by himself. It didn't feel right. Help me, Monika, help me. Don't leave me…

Chapter 15: The Hospital

'Monika, my name is Monika. Does it matter?'

'It's not her that's injured, it's my brother,' added Martin.

The corridor bustled with people, a pair of stretcher-bearers pushed pass them, carrying a small girl huddled in blankets. 'Make way,' they shouted as they zigzagged their way along. Somewhere, someone screamed. The doctor pulled on his goatee. 'You can see how busy we are. There's no way I can leave.'

'But he's in too much pain to move,' said Monika, trying not to lose her patience.

'Then there's nothing we can do. Now, if you'll excuse me…' He turned to leave, tucking a clipboard under his arm.

Monika and Martin looked at each other. Martin shrugged, obviously prepared to accept the doctor's last word. Monika however was not. She ran after him, sidestepping a man on crutches and two women sitting on the floor, leaning against the wall, both quietly crying, one soothing and stroking the hair of the other. 'But tell me, what can I do? He could die there.'

'Look, young lady, I don't know how else to tell you. The hospital is heaving with injuries, half the staff have disappeared and I haven't slept for three days. We've run out of all medicines, antibiotics, chloroform, disinfectants, you name it, everything. We're operating without anaesthetics and for every patient we send home, another five take their place. And you're asking me to leave all this to traipse two kilometres there and two kilometres back to see your boyfriend. In the time I do that, we could lose another twenty. I'm sorry, truly I am, but what do you suggest I do?'

Monika knew she didn't have the answer. The doctor pondered her silence for a few moments. More people passed. Nearby, the two tearful women held on to each other. The doctor scratched his goatee and threw her a look that said this time he didn't expect to be followed. She didn't.

Martin took her hand, 'We did our best.'

She shook his hand off. '*I* did my best. I didn't hear you protest.'

'Oh come on, Monika, look at this place. The doctor's right, you know he is.'

'So what do we do then?'

'Go back to him, keep him warm, keep his spirits up. I'll hunt around the pharmacists and try to find something.'

Another pair of stretcher-bearers rushed by. Monika and Martin leant back against the wall to allow them through. This time, the victim was a middle-aged man, his leg blown off leaving a congealed mesh of bloodied rags.

Monika had seen enough. 'Come on,' she said. 'Let's go.'

*

It felt as if someone was pressing down a huge pile of bricks onto the side of his face. The pressure was unrelenting, the torment constant. Occasionally, a spasm of pain washed over him leaving him exhausted and afraid. The inside of his mouth felt like a cavern as he probed with his tongue, feeling the irregular and alarming contours on the right side. He could still talk but the effort was too much. Swallowing was painful and he hadn't eaten, drinking only water through a straw that Martin had found in a deserted café. He was frightened – frightened of what was going to happen to him, how he was going to get to the hospital. Frightened of the pain to come, frightened of how he looked. The future loomed ahead of him, filling the quiet hours as he lay on his back, staring at the ceiling, and it was no longer a future he could envisage, not one he could look forward to. It had taken a second to shatter the certainties in his life. And nothing would ever be the same again.

He looked around him. He felt imprisoned in the living room that looked as if it could collapse on him at any moment. There were no lights, no glass in the windows, not an inch of surface free of powdery, snow white dust. His body sunk into a bed of white dust within the patchwork quilt. Martin must've have manoeuvred the bed in from the second bedroom. An upturned crate served as a bedside table, bare but for the candles, a half-full packet of cigarettes, a box of matches and, hidden beneath it, a revolver – *for when the Russians come*, Oskar had said. Beside the bed a bottle as a bedpan and a chair frame – the woven seat having disintegrated. The curtain rail had fallen on one side, leaving a trail of curtain, once blue, now dusted and torn. The mantelpiece had caved in, ornaments lying on a heap in front of the grate. Pictures hung at peculiar angles, large chunks of masonry had fallen and were now embedded on the carpeted floor. And everywhere, shards of glass and this all-pervading layer of white dust.

A whole series of needs plagued him, none urgent but together forming a mesh of discomfort and self-pity – the need to urinate, to eat, to drink, to escape this cold. And above all, to rid himself of this pain, this clawing pain that refused to disappear. And lingering beneath it all, the desire to know where Monika was, what was she doing, was she with Martin?

Martin. Never again would anyone confuse the two of them. No longer the need to differentiate the two by the extra mole, the extra smattering of freckles. The difference between them was now as marked as black and white, as beauty and the beast. And he, Peter, the one with the soft heart, the forgiving nature, cast as the beast, the gruesome one. But all the time, his former looks were there to see, to admire. For the rest of his life, he knew whenever he looked at Martin he would see, not his twin, but his own face as it should have been. Whatever was about to happen, he knew that once it was over, he had to escape, to finally break away from his other half, to pretend he'd never existed. He couldn't bear the thought of staring at himself sitting on the other side of the room, bagging the pretty girls that wouldn't give him a glance, enjoying the life that should have been his to share.

A shaft of light stretched across the room, shadows, a familiar voice. She was back. Please God, let her have brought help, something to make this pain go away.

'Peter,' she said, her feet crunching over the shattered glass and masonry.

He wanted to smile but couldn't. Something inside him told him he would never smile again.

'Peter.' Her voice oozed sympathy and concern but within it he could sense the very emotion she was trying so hard to suppress, but he felt it nonetheless, the pity. She sat on the chair without its seat and took his hand and stroked it. 'Oh, Peter, we tried but they won't come.' She told him of the doctor with the goatee, the corridor of distresses, the lack of medicines.

'But Martin is still out searching,' she added, raising her voice to emphasise the optimism she lacked. 'You know Martin, he'll find something.'

Yes, he thought, he knew Martin.

Chapter 16: Reassurance

'He's getting worse. You sure there's nothing?'

'Monika, you know I scoured the whole bloody city. Everything's gone; used up.'

'Look at him, the poor love.' She slid off the chair without its seat and leant against Peter's bed, stroking his hair, studying his face. A face she knew so well. She thought back the nine years to the day in the forest, her sister swimming naked. It'd been the first time she'd spoken to them without the presence of adults. It wasn't the best of starts but since then the three of them had grown up together, protected each other and laughed together. She ran her finger down his left jawbone, across the stubble, and his lips, dried and cracked. How white and aged his skin, she thought, how brittle his hair. And how she missed his perfect face. The bullet had only grazed him, as a passer-by had said, almost convincingly, but the left side of his face was a terrible mess, the cheek pulverised, fissures of flesh, the ridges of congealed blood.

Graze seemed too inadequate a word. And now an infection had set in.

Most of the time he slept, free of the pain that tormented his waking hours. Occasionally he experienced a brief period of conscious calm, free from pain, during which moments he could speak and eat. Monika would break bread into small pieces and feed it to him with sips of water. When she had to leave, she made sure she left food and water on his bedside table – the upturned crate beneath which hid the revolver left behind by Oskar.

She looked up and Martin was still there. He'd been staring down at her all the while. At moments like this she was grateful for his presence and his words of reassurance. Words, she knew, that came only with difficulty but were there, nonetheless. She felt grateful too that the face she missed so much was still so visible in another. She thought of the previous evening, when Martin, for the first time, lay next to his brother and Peter turned to face him. The vision of the two silent brothers, lying on the backs, looking at each other, their noses almost touching, jolted her heart. Until the grazing bullet had done its work, a mirror held upright between them would have had the same effect, one brother gazing at the other and seeing himself. But not now.

At other times, perhaps most of the time, she found herself resenting Martin, resenting his perfect features while Peter's face remained obscured by his mangled wound. Had Martin shown any disquiet while the other half of his soul languished in pain? Had the burden of his brother's injury slowed him down or softened him? No, thought Monika, none of these things had happened. Martin was still Martin, only more so. The identical twins –

match for match in beauty, but God had seen to it that the kind one, the one with the heart should suffer, while his feckless brother revelled in his strength and his being. Even God had got them mixed up.

'I'll go.'

'No, you don't have to.' She knew really that he wanted to go; there was only so much he could take of his brother's presence and her maudlin anxiety.

'He'll be OK.'

She laughed her tearful laugh, and wondered what made him say something so obviously false, so inappropriately bland. Peter was not going to be OK. The infection was spreading, doing its vicious work on his system, and he had neither the strength nor the medication to fight it. Peter was going to be anything but OK.

Chapter 17: The Park

Monika hadn't been out for a couple of days, devoting her time and energy in caring for Peter, who lay motionless, slowly slipping away. She'd cried so much she had nothing left to cry. Martin went out frequently, bringing back bits of food or fuel. Finally, she could bear it no more; she needed air, to escape the suffocation inside that dingy room.

Together with Martin, Monika took a walk, gawking at the chaos that scarred the city, occasionally stopping to read one of the newspapers plastered up on walls or shop fronts. A weak sun filtered through the clouds; people were out on the streets, trying to fathom out what the future held for them. The few remaining optimists clapped each other on the back, saying that Germany wasn't finished yet, that she would fight back and ultimate victory was still to be had; but most people shook their heads and spoke fearfully of the Russians but dared not speak too loud – defeatist talk could have dire consequences. They saw a queue of people outside a post office – people waiting to withdraw their life savings. Reluctantly, they joined the queue. Two hours later, they left, their pockets stuffed with what remained of their money, their accounts closed.

No street was free of corpses; bodies lay statuesque-like, covered in coats, some sprinkled with lime to lessen the pungent aroma. People strolled from one to another, their hands clasped over their mouths, lifting the coats, looking for a loved one.

Martin suggested a stroll in the park and Monika readily agreed, too tired to decide for herself. He spotted three young boys vacate a bench and ran to claim it. Monika joined him, pleased to sit down. They sat in silence and watched a father play football with his two young sons, allowing them to score at frequent intervals amid yelps of delight. Martin laughed and Monika tried to smile

'He's dying, you know.'

'Peter?' She noticed him cast his eyes down, fiddling with a button on his coat. 'Yes,' he said eventually. 'I know.'

'It's only that…'

'Go on.'

'You act as if you don't care.'

Martin sat up and half-turned to face her. 'That's not fair, I do care but…' He slunk back on the bench. 'I do care, Monika, I care a lot; he's my brother and I miss him. But I feel so useless, I can't help him, none of us can.'

One of the small boys fell awkwardly chasing the ball. He lay on the grass, motionless, stunned, before letting loose an ear-piercing scream. His father ran to him and scooped him up in his arms, pressing his face into his and smothering him with concern.

'Do you really miss him?'

'Yes.'

'So do I.'

'I want to say sorry to him, to say sorry for having been such a shit to him all these years.' The words came quickly but he stopped abruptly and cast his eyes heavenwards, grappling with his thoughts. 'It's strange, isn't it, how you don't appreciate something until it's too late?'

'Yes, I know.'

'I mean, we grew up together, he was always there, we came back to Berlin together, we've always lived together. He's always been part of my life. But God, it's more than that; he's *part* of me. I suppose they say that of twins and it's true. I never really thought about it until now but it's so obvious. Martin and Peter, the inseparable twins. And suddenly, he's not there any more, he's lying in that shit-hole with this fucking infection eating him up and I don't know what to do, so I do nothing. But part of me is dying and whatever I do, I can't escape it. So, yes, I miss him.'

Their arms intertwined, their faces touching cheek to cheek.

'We talk of him as if he's already gone.'

Martin laughed, a sorrowful laugh. 'I know.'

Their foreheads touched as they whispered to one another within the privacy of their own shadows. 'I'm sorry, I didn't realise, I thought…'

'You thought I didn't care.'

'I was wrong.'

'Yes, but I understand why you thought it.'

'I miss him too.'

'I was always jealous, you know.'

'Of us two?'

'Yes.'

'You should've beaten him on the tightrope then.'

He laughed again as her words immediately took his mind back six years to the village green, the taste of Coca-Cola on his tongue, the face of Tomi, the quartet of old men with their instruments, his feet poised on the tightrope. He lifted his head a fraction and his lips touched her cheek. He kissed it delicately, kissed the wetness of her face, the stain of tears on her skin. He left his lips there, not wanting to break the moment, not wanting to lose the warmth of her skin against his lips.

'Martin. Martin? We ought to get back.'

'Yes,' he said with a sigh. 'We ought to get back.'

Together, they stood up and the world returned into focus – the park, the bent trees, the craters. As they left, Martin glanced back. The father with his footballing sons had gone.

Chapter 18: Café Von Bismarck

It's strange, thought Monika, how a lifetime's perception of a person can change overnight. She'd never considered before that Martin's swaggering might only be a cover for the real man who lay beneath. And yesterday, in the park, she'd discovered the real man, the real Martin. The twins were more alike than she'd thought. While Peter carried his geniality for all to see, Martin hid it away behind a screen of bravado – but it was still there nonetheless. Her mood lightened and then, as a consequence, soon darkened again. When she thought about this chain of emotion, she knew why – as well as Peter's face, his personality would live on in his brother, albeit in a diluted form, but it meant that through Martin, Peter was expendable.

Peter himself was failing fast but there were still periods when he was conscious and able to elucidate. But these periods were becoming increasingly rare. She did her best to keep him warm, to feed and wash him, to hold his hand. At other times, she scoured the area, still trying to find a doctor, queuing for food, finding fuel.

Martin, as well, was subdued as they ambled aimlessly through the alleyways and avenues. It was as if his admission the previous day had sapped his energy. The fight had left him. They walked what felt like miles through the wounded city, in silence, unable to talk about what happened in the park yet unable to talk about anything else.

More cafés were reopening, the staff having made an attempt to sweep away the glass and the worse of the debris, to shake the tablecloths free of dust, to wash down the counters and machinery, to find new light bulbs to replace the shattered ones. People, thankful for a hint of normality, flocked to the cafes offering half-priced coffee. Monika and Martin sat inside the Café Von Bismarck with its nicotine-stained walls and a low ceiling that gave the place a claustrophobic feel. They took a small table near the doorway and, sitting side by side, nursed their cups of coffee, pleased to rest their feet after walking so long, to feel warm for a while. Behind them, people came and went, a constant stream of customers passing through, the place abuzz with animated conversations, of laughter even, the smell of coffee and tobacco smoke.

Monika watched Martin as he stared into his coffee, his shoulders hunched. She wanted to reach out, to touch him, to reassure him but of what she wasn't sure. How beautiful a man, she thought; his beauty even more striking than before – now that his was the only one.

Martin reached for the sugar bowl and added another spoonful to his coffee. 'What's that brooch?' he asked.

'Oh, this,' she said, looking down at the rose-shaped brooch she'd pinned to her coat. 'It was my sister's. I'm rather fond of it. I wear it occasionally.'

'You know,' he said, stirring, 'it's strange you mentioned the tightrope contest yesterday. Did you care who won?'

Monika stretched her memory back. 'Yes. I wanted Peter to win.'

'Why?'

'I don't know. Perhaps because Peter seemed more manageable. I'm sorry, that sounds silly.'

Martin laughed. 'No, I think I know what you mean. I think we both loved you.'

Monika smiled coyly. 'And perhaps I loved you both.'

'Perhaps you still do.'

His words shocked her not only because of his presumption but because of their accuracy. 'No,' she said in a whisper. 'I don't, it wouldn't be right, I…'

His mouth against hers felt so deliciously natural, so perfect, but she pulled away. It wasn't right, like she'd said, it wasn't right at all. Holding hands under the table, she felt the need to run, to run away from both Martin and his brother. But she knew she couldn't – not now, not ever. She leant against him, feeling his warmth. He put his arm around her. The gesture made her shiver with cosiness. She wanted to drown in his kiss, to float away from all the chaos in the world, such a beautiful, beautiful man. It'd been him, Martin, always had been, the exciting one, the one with fire in his eyes. Oh, Peter, I'm sorry, I don't want to lose you. She loved them both, she didn't want to but she realised now that she did. Martin was right, she always had, always will – Martin and Peter, the beautiful twins, she didn't want to lose them both, couldn't face a life without them, without him, without Martin. She kissed him. Don't leave me, she thought, don't stop kissing me. 'Don't, Martin, don't.'

'Don't what?'

'Don't you leave me too.'

*

With their arms wrapped round each other, they wandered back towards the apartment. Leaning into him for warmth, she didn't want the moment to end, didn't want to face Peter again. She couldn't bear the thought of Peter dominating her thoughts, wanting desperately instead to enjoy the smell and aura of Martin, but Peter's face refused to fade from her mind. And the face she saw was not the Peter she wanted to remember, that face belonged exclusively to Martin now, but the gaunt face of a man being eaten from within.

The pavement was awash with loose stones and rubble; Monika stumbled; Martin scooped her up. Without words, they kissed, blind to passers-by, to people talking, to trucks rumbling along, to newspaper vendors shouting their publications.

'My God,' said Martin suddenly. 'That's Albert.'

'Who's Albert?'

'Don't you remember? Tomi's friend – you know…'

She caught sight of him, hands in pocket, a man scurrying towards them. Yes, she remembered – remembered catching him on Hitler's birthday kissing another boy behind the café while Martin held his bottle of Coca-Cola behind his back. He almost walked into them, muttering an apology.

'Hello, Albert,' said Martin.

The man stopped, his eyes wide with fright. 'Oh, shit, it's you. Peter. Monika.' Monika could see that Martin was about to correct him but decided against it. Albert seemed in no mood to chat and made to leave.

'Hey, hey, Albert, not so fast. Haven't seen you in years.'

'So what?' He tried to step round Martin but Martin blocked him.

'Not so fast, Albert. Not so fast. So, how goes it? What you doing now?'

'What? Do you care?'

'Yeah, I do. Tell me.'

'I've got a job if you must know. An important one.'

'Have you now? An important one? Doing what exactly?'

He looked round as if he was about to divulge a secret. 'If you must know, I work in the Army HQ, Transfers Division.'

Martin's eyes lit up. 'Transfers Division? Well, that's useful to know.'

'Is it?'

'Yes. Yes, indeed.'

'I've got to go. Good to see you both still alive, you never know these days who's going to cop it from one day to the next. How's your brother?'

Martin couldn't help glancing at Monika. 'Not so good, he was hit.'

'Serious?'

'It is now. There's nothing left in the hospitals, and no one will come out to him.'

'Happened to a friend of mine – died for the lack of plasma.'

'He's got a terrible infection,' added Monika. 'It's destroying him.'

'You married, Albert?'

Albert eyed him. 'I really have to go now.'

Martin stepped to one side. 'Yes, yes, of course. You have an important job to get to. I'll pop in and see you some time.'

'I'd rather you didn't.'

Martin watched him leave, stroking his chin.

'What was that about?' asked Monika.

'Hmm? Oh, nothing. Nothing at all.'

Chapter 19: Not Going Back

'I'm not going back.'

'I'm sorry?'

They were in the apartment, in the kitchen with its dingy wallpaper, its linoleum floor, sitting at the table opposite each other, a couple empty dinner plates and mugs pushed to one side. Peter was asleep in the living room. Martin looked up at Monika, holding her gaze. 'I said I'm not going back, back to my unit.'

She tried to speak, unable to comprehend what he was saying.

'I don't care what you think, what anyone thinks. Call me a traitor, a coward, whatever, I don't care. I've done things, Monika, things I'm not proud of, things I know will haunt me for the rest of my life. Yet out there, in the middle of nowhere, the bleakest place you can imagine, snow everywhere, unbelievably cold, shooting a mother and her teenage girl between the eyes seemed… well, if not normal, then certainly acceptable.'

'No, please, Martin. Why are you telling me these things? I don't need to know.'

'Because I thought I was doing it for you, for everyone, for the Fatherland, for the good of the nation. The boys in my unit – one by one I saw them get killed. I knew it was only a matter of time. We measure our lives in years. I was measuring mine by days, then, as we pushed further, by the hour. That's then I knew. We weren't Germany's future; we were its cannon fodder. I saw lieutenants, majors, colonels getting the hell out. Yeah, OK, they pulled a few strings, got themselves transferred, but they knew what they were doing, we all did. If I go back, I'll never see you again, Monika.' He stopped, searching his pockets. With trembling fingers, he lit a cigarette, exhaling the smoke, watching it disperse. 'A year ago, I got hit; a bullet to the calf muscle. Nothing serious. But enough to get me transferred. Fantastic, I thought. I was sent to a camp – guard duty. Easy work while I recuperated. It was a camp for Jews. There were others there too but mainly Jews.'

'Like the concentration camps?'

'No. Worse. Much worse.'

'Worse?'

He shook his head. Monika realised with a jolt that he was crying.

'They were killing them. Hundreds, thousands, every day.'

'The Jews?'

'Gas. They use gas.'

'Gas? How can they…? I don't understand.'

'I saw it with my own eyes, Monika. My own eyes.'

'Why? Why would they… I don't believe you.'

He slammed his fist on the table. The plates and mugs bounced. 'You don't believe me?' he shouted. 'You think I'm making it up?'

'Please, Martin. Please tell me it's not true.'

'I'm not going back, Monika. I can't.'

'You can't not go back; they'd shoot you.'

'And I'd be shot if I go back. So either way, I'm fucked.'

'You could escape.'

'I know. And I know a man who can help.'

Chapter 20: Sirens

Over the next couple of days Monika stayed inside the flat, looking after Peter who drifted in and out of consciousness. He looked worse with each passing day, his skin greyer, flakier, his temperature dangerously high. Applying cold flannels to his brow made little difference. While Peter slept, she busied herself by cleaning the apartment. They still had running water, but she kept the bath full – just in case. Martin spent the days out, where, she had no idea, reappearing only to sleep.

One night, Monika was awoken by the sirens. Jumping out of bed, she grabbed her coat and went to the spare room to find Martin still asleep. She shook him awake. 'Martin, listen, *listen…*'

He sat up on hearing the high-pitched drone of the sirens.

'They're coming back,' said Monika.

Martin rubbed his eyes, it was still only one in the morning but as the noise registered, he leapt from the bed, his eyes wide with panic, and rushed to the window.

'We're going to have get Peter down to the cellar,' said Monika.

Between them, they tried to lift Peter up as the sound of the sirens became steadily louder. 'God, he's heavy,' said Martin breathlessly.

Peter opened his eyes. 'What are you doing?'

Monika stroked his hair. 'Peter, oh, my love. There's going to be an air raid. We've got to get you down to the cellar.'

He heard the sirens. 'No. You two go. Leave me here.'

'Peter, we can't do that, love.'

Martin, more brusquely, told him to get up.

'No, I can't move.'

'Get up, you stupid bastard.'

But Peter, close to tears, his energy sapped, refused to.

They heard the anti-aircraft engage, like that of a rapid barking dog, and beneath it the drone of the planes. 'For fuck's sake, Peter. Look, this is your choice,' shouted Martin. 'Come,' he said, offering Monika his hand. 'Let's get out of here.'

'What? We can't leave Peter here.'

Then came the horrendous noise of the bombs falling, detonating. The walls shook. The lights flickered, then went out. The air pressure intensified, pounding their ears. Martin dived under the table. Monika screamed, covering her ears. Ceiling plaster fell, the floor trembled. Another bomb. Shattered glass flew across the room. The block of apartments opposite collapsed, crashing down as if it'd been built of straw, leaving huge clouds of black smoke amongst the flames. Peter covered his face with his hands, his blanket covered in plaster and shards of glass.

Martin and Monika, grappling on the floor in the pitch dark, bumped into each other. Martin shouted something but what, Monika had no idea, the noise of the planes and the bombs and the explosions ear-splittingly loud. The utter sense of vulnerability reduced her to tears. Crying, she fell into his arms, curled up in his lap, shivering with fear. As more bombs fell, she gripped Martin's arm, aware of her fingernails biting into his flesh. She felt the sudden stab of anger coarse through her – anger that, through his stubbornness, Peter should have exposed them to this; they were going to die here, in this blackness, their mouths and nostrils bunged up with dust, their ears deafened by the intensity of noise. Martin pressed her head against his chest, stroked her hair.

Then, almost as sudden as it had started, there came a lull. The ceiling light bulb flickered back into life exposing a room almost white with powdery dust.

'Please, God, let there be no more,' she whimpered.

'I think they've gone,' said Martin, his chin resting on her head. 'You all right, Peter?' he called out.

Peter, coughing, managed to splutter a 'yes'.

They remained where they were, too frightened, too dazed to move. The minutes ticked by. The city outside, through the broken windows, remained eerily quiet, just the ominous sound of buildings on fire, of masonry and timber collapsing.

Eventually, came the sound of the all-clear. Disentangling themselves, Martin and Monika clambered to their feet, rustling their hair, wiping away the worse of the dirt and dust.

Monika attended to Peter, taking water from the bath in a pan, using a flannel to clean him, while Martin looked round the apartment, surveying the damage. 'Could have been a lot worse,' was his considered opinion.

'Leave me next time,' said Peter, his voice coarse and quiet. 'I'm dying–'

'Peter–'

'I know I am. But you have to save yourself. Please, next time…'

Chapter 21: Passes

The following day, Martin returned to the apartment, looking pleased with himself. Monika was in the living room, using a tea towel to sweep the dust and bits of plaster off the table. Peter lay fast asleep.

'I went to see Albert today,' he said, rubbing his hands against the cold.

'What for?'

'He's doing us a little favour.'

'Is he? Like what?'

'We're going to Switzerland, we can't stay here.'

'Switzerland? Are you mad?'

Her words stopped him in his tracks. 'Monika,' his voice quiet. 'Monika, I told you – I'm not going back. The war is lost; everyone knows that. Everyone except the diehard fanatics. Once the Russians get here, we'll be as good as dead, that is unless the Brits don't get us first.'

'No. That stuff about the Russians, they say it's just government propaganda, that it won't be that bad.'

'After what we've done to them? They'll be out for revenge, Monika. If we stay, they'll kill me and Peter, that's for sure, and they'll rape you.'

'Rubbish. You're just saying that to frighten me. What do we do about Peter?'

'Leave him.'

'I don't believe you can mean that.'

He threw his scarf onto a chair. 'We have no choice.'

This was the side of Martin she didn't like, the arrogance of the dominant brother – no hesitation, no second thought, simply the dogged belief that what he said was right. But Peter was in no state to offer his opinion – it was down to her.

'I won't leave without him.'

'He's dying, Monika, we can't take him.'

'Then I won't leave at all.'

He pounced on her with such force she fell back against the wall. The memory flashed through her mind – pushed against the tree near the lake so many years ago. 'For fuck's sake, the time for heroics is over.' A splay of spittle doused her face; she'd never heard him so high pitched. 'We'll be slaughtered, we *have* to leave.'

'He's right, Monika.' The voice so weak seemed to come from somewhere faraway.

They halted as if caught in a freeze frame, Martin's hands grasping her by the shoulders.

'Peter,' she cried. Shrugging Martin off, she went to him and placed her hand on his forehead. 'How are you feeling?'

'OK, I guess.'

'You are, Brother?'

Struggling to pull himself up, Peter answered breathlessly. 'Better than ever.'

Monika tried not to wince from the stench of his breath. 'Martin thinks we should leave.'

'I know, I heard.'

'But we can't leave you.'

Peter smiled a ghostly smile. 'I think I could do it, I feel OK.' Monika shot a doubtful look at Martin. Peter caught it. 'Believe me,' he said. 'Just get me to a train and I'll be all right.'

'That's right,' said Martin. 'And once we're in Switzerland, we'll be able to get you some proper attention.' Monika wondered whether Martin was serious or, as she feared, merely placating him. Outside, a fire engine, its siren full blast, made its way down the street. Martin reached for his coat. 'I'll have to go and see Albert again – if it's not too late.'

She watched him leave, trying to squash the sense of disappointment that he hadn't said goodbye, not even a look of acknowledgement. Instead, she took Peter's hand, wishing she knew what she wanted.

*

Hours later, Monika's heart leapt as the door burst open. Instinctively, she reached for the revolver hidden beneath the upturned crate next to Peter's bed, and breathed a sigh of relief when she saw Albert standing at the doorway. She put the revolver back.

'Is Peter here?' he asked.

She was about to point to Peter in the bed, but realised he meant Martin. 'No,' she said.

'Here.' He threw an envelope on the table. 'I've done my bit. Tell him I don't expect to see him again.'

'What's that?'

'Your passes.'

'Our passes?'

'I signed them off. It gives you and him official permission to travel to Munich. I didn't want him coming again to the office, hence this personal delivery. How kind am I? I guess Switzerland is not too far from there – if that's what you want. I don't want to know. As Peter's officially classed as an invalid, it wasn't too difficult. I put you down as his carer. What you do once you're in Munich is not my problem.'

Monika glanced nervously at Peter who'd drifted back asleep and hoped he was sleeping soundly. 'Did Martin, I mean Peter... did Peter come see you about a third pass?'

'No. Anyway, that'd be pushing it. I wouldn't be able to wrangle that much.' He stepped over to the bed. 'So,' he said, peering inquisitively down at Peter. 'What happened to Martin? Christ, he looks awful.'

'He was wounded. Eastern Front.' How easily came the falsehood. 'Shush, you'll wake him.'

But it was too late; Peter opened his eyes and saw Albert standing over him. 'Albert? What... I don't understand... what passes? What are you doing here?'

'You mean, they're going to leave you behind?'

'What?'

'Ask your brother. I can't hang around.'

As he was about to leave, the door swung open again, and there stood Martin, breathless, his hair dishevelled. 'Did you get them?' he asked on seeing Albert.

Albert pointed at the table.

He picked up the envelope, inspecting the passes inside. 'Good man,' he said. 'Your secret's safe with me, my friend.'

'Fuck you.' And with that, he was gone.

'It's like an inferno out there,' said Martin, removing his coat. 'Bodies everywhere. Everyone's talking about the Ivans. They're terrified and they have every right to be.'

'How did you get Albert to obtain those passes?' asked Monika. 'What secret?'

'It's all about what you know,' he said, tapping his nose. 'The Party still frowns on homosexuals, don't they?'

'You blackmailed him?'

'Yeah. So what?'

'I can't leave Peter.'

Martin sat down next to Monika, both next to Peter's bed. They didn't dare look at each other. Monika's mind spun and yet no thoughts formed, only the booming of her heart. After a while, she got up. 'You need a wash, Peter; I'll boil up some water,' she said, trying not to let her voice betray the shame simmering inside her.

'He thought I was you.' The softly spoken words hung accusingly in the air.

'Albert? No, he got you confused,' said Monika, standing next to the stove.

'Like when we were kids,' said Martin. 'We're used to that, aren't we, Brother?' Martin tried to add a chortle but it came across contrived.

'We need to get you cleaned up,' said Monika.

'He got confused,' repeated Martin.

'We're not so easy to confuse nowadays.' He swallowed, his Adam's apple bobbing up and down. 'So, you're escaping. Both of you. Using my name as an invalid. I remember Oskar saying to me that I had to get Monika away before the Russians arrive. But what about me?'

'He couldn't get us another. I tried, honestly, Peter, I tried.'

Peter reached out towards the upturned crate.

'Want a hand?' said Martin, still sitting next to the bed.

'No, I only need some water.' With that, he leant over, and in one movement pushed the crate over – the plate, mug and ashtray falling noisily to the floor – and scooped up the revolver.

'Peter?'

Monika came over from the stove. 'Peter, you don't need that, love.'

He held the gun lightly in his hand. 'No?' Then, with tears clouding his eyes, he spoke quickly, painfully. 'You didn't try – I heard him. You're just going to leave me here. Funny thing is, I don't blame you. But don't worry, I'm not going to let the Russians get me. What upsets me is that you're using me, my name, my disability as your ticket out of here. I've always played second fiddle to you, haven't I, Martin? You remember, as kids? We always did what you said, went where you wanted to go; you never thought to ask me because my opinion didn't count. You know, I've often wondered about your conscience and over the years and I've come to the conclusion you don't have one.

'Do you remember Miss Hoffman? It was you all the time, wasn't it? She liked me more than you and you couldn't bear that. So, you got your little revenge, shopped her for daring to utter an anti-Nazi thought. I only hope she survived, that she's out there now, living and surviving.

'And the play. You remember that, of course. You resented it because I got the better part – even if was just the one line. I hated you for not admitting your sabotage. I got caned but you could have saved me – but no, why would you want to?'

His tears had made rills through the dirt on his face. 'Monika was my one victory over you, and all because I had the better balance. And how you must've hated that. But even I didn't know quite how much it rankled. How long was it? Five, five and a half years? And then she succumbed. How did you do it, Martin? Showed her your softer side, tried to merge the two of us into one, so she'd fall for the Peter in you? I hate you, Martin; I never knew how much I hated you until now. Funny, isn't it, how people assume we're the same just because we are on the outside. But in the inside, we couldn't be less alike. I reckon we've always hated each other without really realising it. But it's over now; we don't have to face it any more. Either I shoot you now or you walk out that door for Switzerland and never come back. Which is it? Tell me, Martin, tell me what to do, one last time.'

'I will. Let me go, let me take Monika with me. You know what will happen to her if I don't.'

'Martin, stop,' cried Monika. 'Stop, just stop.' She thought she was yelling but the words emerged as barely a whisper. 'I won't leave Peter.'

'He's right though,' said Peter. 'I… want…' A fit of coughing took hold. Clutching his chest with one hand and the revolver in the other, he coughed and wheezed.

Monika stroked his hair. 'You OK, Peter? I'm staying right here; I won't leave you.'

'No. I'd rather you fell into Martin's clutches than a Russian's.'

Martin rose carefully to his feet, aware of the revolver in his brother's shaking hands. 'Maybe you're right, Peter, maybe everything you say is right. I admit, I am a selfish sod, I can't help it. I admit it, I did denounce Miss Hoffman; I did plan to steal Monika away from you, exactly as you said. But there's something you've got wrong. I don't hate you; I love you, you stupid bastard, you're my brother, I shall always love you...'

'Do I believe you, Martin?'

'Yes, Peter, you do.'

'Perhaps I do. Save her, then. Take her with you; get her out of here.'

Martin nodded. He leant down and kissed his brother on his brow.

'Be brave,' he whispered in his brother's ear. 'You can do it.'

'Peter... please.' Monika paced up and down, scrunching her hair.

'I can't help you, Monika. Only Martin can help you now. But please, go now. Don't make it worse.'

Martin disappeared to the bedroom, returning moments later with his army rucksack. 'I took the liberty to pack a few things. Bit of food, a few clothes, underwear. Not much, mind you. We don't want to give the impression we're not coming back.' He scooped up the passes from the table, picked up his coat and took Monika's. 'I'm going to go now. It could take the whole day to get on a train. Monika, please, let's do this now.'

With tears in her eyes, biting her hand, she looked down at Peter.

Peter nodded at her. 'Please go. Please.'

She stepped towards him, as if wanting to embrace him. But she stopped – she knew if she touched him, she'd never let go. 'Goodbye, my love.'

'Go, please. Go now.'

And so, with her heart aching with pain and shame, she followed Martin out of the apartment, closing the door behind her.

They passed Jünger, the block warden on the stairs. 'You two going somewhere?' he asked. Monika kept her head down, not wanting Jünger to see her crying.

'Taking provisions to my aunt,' said Martin. 'She's poorly.'

'Right then; you'd better hurry.'

Outside, the sun shone upon the devastated street, the piles of rubble, blackened houses, the ruination of a city. Everywhere, people scurried around, dazed, fatigued faces. Buildings smouldered, smoke lingered. 'City of the damned,' muttered Martin. 'Come.' He offered Monika his hand. She took it. 'It'll take a good hour to get to the station.' With a final glance up at their apartment window, he guided her away.

Carefully, stepping over debris and around holes, they left the block behind them.

They'd only walked half way down the street when Monika stopped abruptly. 'Martin, I forgot my sister's brooch. I can't–'

'No, you can't go back for it.'

Flinging off his hand, she made to return. Martin called after her. She didn't stop. Swearing under his breath, he made to catch her up. Encumbered by his rucksack, tripping over a couple of bricks, he lost ground. By the time he caught her up, they were back outside the apartment block.

'Monika, no...' They heard it — the sound of the single shot from inside. Monika, her hands on her cheeks, looked up at their window. She screamed. The world stopped, fell silent, then drew breath and started again. Losing balance, she fell against Martin, a booming voice in her head asking what that unfamiliar feeling was.

And then, burrowing her face into his shirt, she knew. It was the feeling of her heart breaking.

Chapter 22: The Border

It was eleven at night. In a cramped sitting room in a small house in the middle of endless fields, sat Martin and Monika, hoping to make good their escape over the border and into Switzerland. The old man of the house had gone off to fetch his nephew. The nephew's name, the old man told them, was Hans. For all their reichsmarks, he would guide Martin and Monika to freedom.

The room was dark but warm, a few hard chairs and a wooden table, everything small but solid. In the corner an old sunken armchair. They were too tired, too anxious to talk, conserving their energy for the last treacherous road that lay ahead of them. The old lady provided them each with beef soup and bread followed by a cup of black coffee, gut-wrenchingly strong. They thanked her and afterwards felt better. Martin smoked. They smiled a little at one another. Ahead of them lay the last leg of their journey that would determine their future. Their whole lives depended on the hours ahead and the last three or so kilometres that separated them from the prison that was their country and freedom in Switzerland, a foreign land. Two nations, side by side, but a world apart. Monika wondered whether Martin had given any thought to never seeing Peter again, to never seeing his parents again. She feared he hadn't.

The old man returned, his face lost under whiskers and a huge, rimmed hat. With him a younger man, his nephew, Hans, with a sharp, pointed face and a long clean-shaven chin.

Martin gave Hans all he had – almost twenty reichsmarks. Enough money to keep a family in Berlin going for two months or more. But it didn't matter – they wouldn't be able to change it and the money would be worthless in a new country. Hans thanked them and said it was time to go. Their hearts lurched.

Monika and Martin thanked him, they thanked the old man, and when the old lady came for their dishes, they thanked her too – again.

'Now,' said Hans, 'as soon as we're outside, no talking. Total silence. Keep close to me and when I crouch, you crouch; if I crawl, you crawl. When I wish you good luck, you'll be on your own. You understand?'

'How will we know where to go once you've gone?' asked Monika.

'You'll know.'

Two heads nodded.

'Martin, before we go,' whispered Monika.

'What?'

'Did you really inform on Miss Hoffman?'

He nodded.

'And the play?'

He nodded again, grimacing.

Together, with Hans, they left the warm house and stepped out into the cold and the rain, feeling like soldiers about to go into battle. The task that lay ahead was no less daunting.

Their eyes adjusted to the dark. It was now almost midnight. Tomorrow, they hoped, would truly see a new dawn.

THE END

Rupertcolley.com

Made in the USA
Middletown, DE
17 August 2020

15591001R00087